To Eddie

Best Wishes

David McCadden

David McCaddon is an IT systems consultant who has worked in computing for over 40 years and has spent the past 32 years specialising in Law Enforcement Computer Systems Development. His investigative systems experience has seen him working with police forces worldwide.

To Joan, Simon, Karen and Jake, for all your love,
support and encouragement.

David McCaddon

FOLLOWING DIGITAL FOOTPRINTS

AUSTIN MACAULEY
PUBLISHERS LTD.

A CIP catalogue record for this title is available from the British Library.

ISBN 978 1 78612 488 3 (Paperback)
ISBN 978 1 78612 489 0 (Hardback)
ISBN 978 1 78612 490 6 (E-Book)

www.austinmacauley.com

First Published (2016)
Austin Macauley Publishers Ltd.
25 Canada Square
Canary Wharf
London
E14 5LQ

A huge thank you to Annabelle Hull for your friendship and support in helping me to create this novel; it could not have been achieved without your help and guidance, it is so very much appreciated.

PROLOGUE

He collected the hire car as arranged with the rental company. He completed the paper work, paid in cash and drove off, heading down the M6 southbound. He continued onto the M1 as far as Junction 14, which was sign-posted Milton Keynes and Newport Pagnell.

He toured a number of Business Parks until he found exactly what he was looking for – an identical make, model, colour and year of the hire car. He noted the number plate and headed back up the motorway towards the North West.

Two hours later he was driving through the rainy Manchester streets and soon the car was in the lock-up garage.

From here he caught the train home – but not before tapping the car registration into his iPad and obtaining the VIN/Chassis number of the donor car.

CHAPTER 1

Tim Ridgway drove into the Midshire Police HQ car park that morning in his battered 1992 Red Citroen AX and looked anxiously for a parking bay. He thought it was a wonder the force hadn't impounded the car before now – but they were busy with other matters. He'd thought about parking it around the corner out of sight but innate laziness deterred him from walking in. He parked it up against the wall in a place where at least it was out of sight. He locked it, not because he expected anyone to steal it, but to make sure that the police couldn't get in it to examine it.

The thought crossed his mind that he really must get the tyres sorted out but he had other, more pressing, things on his mind that day. Tim was twenty-five, single and lived in a poor, shabby, one-bedroomed flat just outside the city centre.

He made his way into the Force Computer department where he worked as an IT support technician on the help desk. He was disillusioned with his job, dealing at times with some of the most boring tasks imaginable. But at least it paid better than most jobs. He had gradually over time lost patience – and his temper – with some of the force personnel and often remarked to his colleagues that some of these users shouldn't be allowed out, never mind having access to computer keyboards.

Tim had worked at Midshire Police for two years, having graduated with a first-class Honours Degree in Computer Science. He was a loner. Both his parents had died in a car crash when he was just twelve years old. His grandmother looked after him until he was sixteen and since then he had had to fend for himself. From a young age he'd always wanted to be involved with technology. He'd moved on from playing computer games and had always been intrigued as to how they were developed. As a youngster he had an over-enquiring mind, and was always taking things apart to see how they actually worked. He also had a yearning to develop computer solutions, the chance for which he was not likely to be offered at Midshire, as all their development was done by the various external computer software houses who provided their in-force applications.

He had now progressed from writing his own computer games and started in his spare time to develop software for the police, such as the odd Incident Recording application or Duty Rostering solution. He thought he was doing them a favour – but instead of being praised for his innovations his only reward was to be reprimanded several times. But Tim had now discovered other plans for making money out of hours. He had recently joined a cyber group online forum. He was at the top of the slippery slide into crime.

Then one day, as he trudged into the office and sat at the help desk, he suddenly couldn't understand why everyone seemed to be so busy. Instead of buzzing with the usual chatter or discussion of the latest football news, the room was silent. You could hear a pin drop.

He logged into the support administrators' account and began to plough through the support emails, most of which had been responded to, and already dealt with, by the overnight shift. He was in the process of responding to an email from a user who had forgotten her password to the Vehicle Fleet Management system when an urgent priority email popped up on his screen from Superintendent Jackson, the head of the force IT Department. Tim was requested to attend a meeting at 9.30 prompt in Jackson's office. Before he could wonder why he had been summoned, he received a phone call from the Superintendent's secretary, Samantha Newing, making sure that he had received the message. Could this be the promotion he was hoping for after all this time? Maybe they had finally recognised his talents – he had surely shown his development capabilities and skills? Or perhaps it was simply to praise him for his efforts in the re-install of the Crime Analysis software [which had gone amazingly smoothly].

From the first day he'd set foot in the Computer Department Tim's relationship with his boss had been far from good. Superintendent Jackson was a smart well-dressed gentleman. Ex-army – he was your typical Sergeant Major material whose booming voice indicated a man who would not take any nonsense. He definitely never took no for an answer. He seemed to have developed a catchphrase for when something couldn't be done. "Why!" he would shout and when given the reason he would ask again, "Why?" There was no doubt that Superintendent Jackson always got things done – and on time. Although he did not have a technical background you couldn't bullshit him even if you tried. Tim and the "super" were chalk and cheese. Tim was an untidy, stubborn, scruffy sort of individual and the two of them frequently clashed in meetings.

On the other hand, however, Superintendent Jackson appreciated Tim's IT skills in solving problems quickly and efficiently. It was a good example of a love-hate relationship.

He made his way up the stairs where he was surprised to see another senior police officer whom he did not know sitting there, clearly also attending the meeting.

'Good morning, Tim. Please sit yourself down. Can I introduce you to Chief Inspector Newton from the Professional Standards Department?' said Superintendent Jackson sternly.

Tim nodded and sat down. It seemed like an absolute lifetime before Chief Inspector Newton, who was deep in thought, eventually broke the silence.

'Good morning, Tim,' he said, while browsing through a folder and shuffling his papers. 'You must be wondering why we have called you into the office this morning?'

'Good morning, sir. Yes, I have no idea,' said Tim, who by now was feeling rather anxious.

'Well, look Tim, I'll come straight to the point. I won't beat about the bush. It's been brought to our attention that over the past four weeks you have been accessing and obtaining details from the Police National Computer. I'm sure I don't need to remind you that accessing the highly sensitive PNC without authority is a case of serious misconduct. These details that you have obtained through accessing VODS (Vehicle Online Descriptive Search) include lists of vehicle owners, addresses and registrations.'

'The Midshire Police expects its staff to behave in a professional manner, ethically and with the highest of integrity at all times. Any instance where the conduct of our staff brings the Midshire Police Force into disrepute is treated extremely seriously, in line with our force policy. Did it not occur to you that everything is audited in this organisation and in particular the PNC?' asked the Chief Inspector, leafing through his paperwork.

Tim went white. 'Well, I hadn't realised it was that serious, sir. I assure you it won't happen again.'

Suddenly the tone of the meeting had changed.

'Yes, you are quite right, Ridgway, it certainly won't be happening again, as you will not have access to it. I have been going through your personnel record from HR which does not make for attractive reading, I assure you. Taking into account your previous disciplinary warnings, the report on you, in particular from Superintendent Jackson, and the seriousness of this incident, you leave us with no option – and, as from today, you are dismissed from the force. The HR department will be in touch with your termination arrangements. I suggest you now go back to your desk and clear it immediately, hand in your security pass to Superintendent Jackson and leave the premises. I have already arranged with the systems administrators to remove your security usernames and passwords,' said the Chief Inspector.

'Before you go, would you mind telling us what exactly you were doing with these vehicle details?' enquired Superintendent Jackson.

'It was just curiosity,' replied Tim, as he got up and started walking out of the office. Under his breath he muttered, 'Tossers!' as he returned to the support office.

He went over to his desk and in silence emptied the contents of his drawers into a carrier bag. He ripped the sign saying 'Welcome to the Information Super Highway – Cobbled Section' from his partition wall and discarded it in the rubbish bin. He didn't say anything to his colleagues, who kept their heads down if they were not on the telephone. He made his way to the car park but not before he had collected the fluffy gonks he had previously distributed in the Crime Section.

CHAPTER 2

DC Jack Hodgson had just returned to his office in the Divisional HQ after attending two weeks on the XIM Investigation Management System Course in Altrincham. He'd been with the force for eighteen years, having joined as a cadet. He'd taken his sergeant's examination twice – and failed it miserably both times, and was now resigned to the fact he would always have the rank of constable. Since moving into CID as a Detective Constable he had never been happier than when dealing with some sort of an investigation. As well as being happily married he was the proud father of a boy aged twelve and a girl of nine. He'd been with the Major Incident Team working as a Holmes researcher for the past two years and had impressed the SIOs with his tenacity, his thirst for knowledge and above all his capability in drilling into data. For DC Hodgson searching data was a natural talent which he certainly had in abundance.

'How did the course go, Jack? Bit of a jolly was it?' came the shout from DS Webster, who was standing behind his desk busy placing folders in his briefcase.

'Excellent course, thanks Sarge, but it was far from a jolly, I assure you! It was hard work I can tell you – but at least the lunches were good, I learnt a lot and I can't wait to put the new case management system through its paces. It certainly will save us a massive amount of effort. I can't wait to see how it performs in the force.'

'Well, it may be some time before that happens. Since the Police and Crime Commissioner announced in the press that we have acquired a new force investigation system, believe it or not, everywhere has gone remarkably quiet. The criminals, it appears, have gone underground. In fact you could say it's been the best deterrent we've ever had. At least it gives us time to open up and investigate some of the cold cases again. Look, I must shoot off. I'll be back after lunch, so tell me all about it then. I have an urgent appointment with Detective Superintendent Blanchflower – and you know what he's like if I turn up late!' And DS Webster hurriedly left the office.

'Give Crazy Horse my regards,' said DC Hodgson to himself as he poured himself a coffee and grabbed a biscuit from DS Webster's personal supply.

DC Hodgson went over to his desk, switched on his computer, logged into his account and pulled up his emails. It seemed ages before the Inbox of the force email system eventually appeared.

'Good God! Two hundred and thirty emails to wade through, and most of them crap, I suspect,' he muttered to himself. 'I don't even know where to start on this bloody lot.'

Just then, and without warning, DCI Bentley came into the office. 'Stand by your bed, Hodgson,' he shouted at the top of his voice.

DC Hodgson jumped up and, with a mouthful of biscuit mumbled, 'Good morning, sir. I didn't see you arrive. Can I get you a coffee?'

'No thanks, Hodgson. I like to spring the element of surprise! I trust you enjoyed your investigation system course? Well, believe it or not, I have a nice little job for you, something you can get your teeth into. You've had that nice cushy couple of weeks relaxing so let's see how you get on with what I have in mind. Let's see what this new system of ours can do,' said DCI Bentley, rubbing his hands.

Oh God, thought DC Hodgson. I've seen his idea of nice little jobs before. DCI Bentley had once had him working undercover in the drugs squad as part of a cross-force enquiry. He'd had to dress as a hippy and trail a gang in a caravan believed to be carrying a large amount of drugs with them through deepest East Anglia, only to discover they were a legitimate family on holiday from the Netherlands looking for a suitable place on the Norfolk broads to spread their grandfather's ashes.

'Now then, Hodgson,' thundered DCI Bentley as he paced up and down in front of a map of the area, 'for some time now the force has had a number of car thefts, but the situation on our patch in particular appears to be getting worse. These are no ordinary TWOC (Taking Without Owner's Consent) thefts, but car rental non-returns. In fact the car hire companies didn't even report them at first – for some strange reason. I can't think why. Maybe they didn't want the publicity. Anyway, we need to get to the bottom of this, so let's see what this new system can throw up. Here is the file so far.' And the DCI handed him a large bundle of papers from his briefcase.

'Presumably we issued warrants for arrest on the people hiring these vehicles?' replied DC Hodgson, scanning through the folder.

'Yes, we certainly did on those that were reported – but that's another thing. We can't trace any of them. Let me have your initial findings report by the end of the week and bring in any resource you need. Let's see what that new system does with this lot,' said the DCI as he turned to leave the office.

'Yes, sir, I will get down to it straight away. Something, as you say, I can actually get my teeth into,' said DC Hodgson, relieved that he didn't have to wade through a pile of emails, but nevertheless daunted by the bundle of papers now occupying most of his desk.

CHAPTER 3

He waited until darkness and when there was no-one in sight he walked over to the lockup. He opened the door as quietly as possible, closed it behind him and switched on the light.

He went over to the workbench and, using a small hammer and letter punches, proceeded to press out seventeen letters and numerals on a metal plate. He then opened the bonnet and using a strong adhesive, glued the metal plate over the VIN Chassis Plate on the front of the engine compartment.

He then closed the bonnet and opened the front passenger door, took out the road tax licence disc and amended the registration. Finally he replaced the number plates, brushed the interior, dusted the dashboard and steering wheel and locked the car. He locked the garage door. Soon he would be driving the car on the M74 into Scotland.

CHAPTER 4

Tim Ridgway was now planning the next phase of his life. 'Who wants to work in that crummy old office anyway,' he thought. As far as he was concerned he'd overstayed his welcome and he was far better off out of there. Already he could see ways of earning far more than he had ever dreamt of in the police force.

Now wearing his hooded top, dark jeans and black trainers he made his way down the Oxford Road into the Jelly Bean internet coffee bar. He ordered himself a cappuccino and sat by the window with his back to the wall. It was a good time to go there. The place was normally swarming with students who were keen to keep in touch with their families and friends on the internet, but on this Tuesday mid-morning it was empty. Soon he was logged in as 'Thunderbird2' to the dark web and routed via the remote servers in Singapore and Germany. He accessed the dark troll forum and quickly found what he was looking for – the link to the dark market where cyber crooks could buy and sell items quite happily online globally with the bitcoin currency. He confirmed his order and transferred bitcoins to the user known only as 'Ghost Orchid' for three skimming devices and two pin pads. 'This will do for starters,' he thought. 'If I can get these delivered to the café here by the end of the week, I can have them set up by next Monday morning.'

He'd planned every last detail with his mate Charlie, who would set the petrol station up, and he would install the others at two ATMs, one at the corner shop and the other outside the Co-op around the corner from his flat.

But before that he had other business to attend to. He needed to think through his revenge plan.

***

Wojek Kolowski pushed open the estate agents' door in the High Street, Crewe.

'Good morning, sir, and how can I help you on this very fine morning?' said the assistant cheerily.

'I'm looking to purchase a property in the area, terraced with three bedrooms. It must be already modernised, with a small garden if possible. Up to a maximum of £95,000 and preferably vacant and ready to move into,' said Wojek.

'Well, that shouldn't be a problem. I'll see what we have on the books. You've picked a good time as it's a buyers' market at present. In the meantime, please take a seat and I'll be with you shortly. Would you like a tea or a coffee?'

'No, but thank you anyway,' replied Wojek.

'Very well, I shouldn't be too long,' said the assistant, going off to the filing cabinets.

Wojek took a seat over by the window and busied himself looking through an impressive folder of references and letters from satisfied customers.

Five minutes later the assistant was back with a dozen property sheets. 'I think you will find these of interest,' she said, handing him the sheets. 'There are three properties which are vacant and actually ready to move into without a chain, and if you wish to view any of these then please don't hesitate to call us. Here is my business card. We will be delighted to show you around. Have you just moved into the area, Mr…?'

'Yes, you could say that. Thank you ever so much. I'll get back to you later to arrange a viewing,' he said, declining to give his name.

'Strange man,' she thought as he got up and left, closing the door behind him.

***

DC Hodgson was now deeply engrossed in the mound of paperwork relating to the stolen vehicles. There had been at least ten vehicles hired from various car rental companies which had not been returned over the past six months. The latest ones seemed to be involving a number of Ford Mondeos – but that could have been pure coincidence. Two had been found abandoned and they had subsequently been returned, so he discounted those and added them to his low priority folder. The annoying thing was that the abandoned ones had been recovered rather rapidly by the rental companies and cleaned before the SOCO guys could even get to see them. The others had completely disappeared without trace.

There's no obvious pattern to this, he thought, other than the make and model – and maybe that's just because it's the most popular hire car. He started keying the data directly into XIM and also pulled down and imported all the vehicle crime and associated offender data from the Crime System for the previous twelve months. Soon he realised he had made a mistake as he was now swamped in a sea of data and was trying desperately to make sense of it all to see the full picture.

He realised that this was going to be a long job and was unsure where to start. He badly needed assistance, and in particular an analyst, to help him see through the maze of links and connections and make sense of it all. He remembered when he was on the 'link analysis for detectives' course how bringing all the data into your workspace could generate a ball of string and wasn't always the wisest move. He'd already co-opted into the team DC Bradley and Ted Wilson, a civilian indexer, to help him. He'd worked with both of them before and they trusted each other implicitly. This was not going to be a quick overnight detection by any means. He picked up the phone and called the MIT office manager.

'Hello sir, I'm sorry to trouble you, but this is DC Hodgson. I am working on a complex case which we are investigating under Operation Carousel. We are working out of Broomfields, the old police training college. The case is particularly protracted and I need an analyst full time to work with us. Do you have anyone you could loan to us as part of our investigation team for a few weeks?'

'I do indeed,' came the reply from DI Harrison. 'And when would you need this analyst?'

'As soon as possible, preferably tomorrow.'

'Tomorrow! Are you bleeding joking, Hodgson? You're having a laugh aren't you! What do you think this is – some sort of a temp recruitment agency?'

'No, sir, sorry sir. I realise it is very short notice but I've been asked by DCI Bentley to set up the investigation and pull in whatever resources I need.'

'Good heavens! The impossible I can do now, but miracles take a little longer. Let me think. Now, yes I can send Jean Price over to you in the morning. She is one of our top analysts who has just finished a case which is awaiting a court date, so she'll be ideal. But I'll need her back when we have the date, mind. Now, look after her. She's one of our best people, and I don't want you lot getting her into bad ways and teaching her bad habits. And keep her out of those pub lunches you have! All right?'

DC Hodgson wondered how DI Harrison knew about the pub lunches. He was clearly getting a bit of a reputation in the force. He must watch that.

'Yes sir, certainly sir, and thanks for your quick response. I owe you one.' And DC Hodgson put the phone down and started building his case file.

CHAPTER 5

'Come in, come in! Please sit yourself down. Can I get you a tea – or a coffee perhaps?'

Mr Hancock, the bank manager, eased himself into his leather armchair, which seemed much higher than the chair on which Wojek was seated. Wojek could not help noticing the presence of a CCTV camera in the corner of the office.

'No, thank you. I am fine.'

Wojek felt somewhat uneasy in his chair.

'So, how can we help you, erm, Mr Kolowski isn't it?'

Mr Hancock leant back in his chair.

'Well, I'd like to arrange a mortgage on a property I've seen in the Crewe area. I have recently moved here from Poland to work as a bricklayer on a large building project in the area. I have already had a survey done – which is fine – and completed the application forms as your assistant at the counter requested.'

Wojek carefully handed over the paperwork.

'Right. Yes, I can see you've been very busy. Now, let me see if we have everything we need at this point.'

Mr Hancock studied the application forms.

'I see you wish to borrow £85,000, you have a cash deposit of £10,000, and your annual income is £45, 000,' said Mr Hancock, peering over his glasses and looking

27

down his nose in what Wojek thought was a somewhat arrogant fashion.

'Yes, that's right. I have saved over the years and my family are very excited to be joining me in the area once we have our own place.'

'So, is it your intention to live here permanently, Mr Kolowski?'

'Oh, yes. We are very much looking forward to settling here in the North West.'

'And where are your family at present, Mr Kolowski? Are they already in this country?'

'No, they are all staying at my mother's in Warsaw.'

'I see. And do you have any references from your employer that we can see?'

'Yes, I have them with me here.'

Wojek handed over a photocopy of a letter.

'Well, everything does seem to be in order – but I will need to send these off to our head office. At first glance I cannot see any problem with this application. It should take us about a week and I will contact you as soon as we have the go-ahead. I assume we can get in touch with you on this mobile number? You will of course need to have a current account with us – but we can set that up when you come in to do the paperwork for the mortgage. Is there anything else that we can help you with, Mr Kolowski?'

'Yes, there is actually. I assume, Mr Hancock, that when we have the current account set up, both my wife and I can have a credit card?'

'Oh, but of course, yes. I am sure we can accommodate that for you. It will, however, be around three months before everything is established, which I'm sure you understand.'

'Thank you very much, sir. I look forward to hearing from you.'

Tim Ridgway had collected the parcel from the Jelly Bean café early that morning and he was now making his way back through the pouring rain to his run-down flat in Crumpsall Street. There was no way he was going to have the parcel addressed to his place for fear of it being traced to him – and he was still feeling somewhat paranoid after his dismissal. He had a good thing going with Alan, the owner of the Jelly Bean, whose address he could use whenever he liked – in return for one or two favours. He made a quick phone call on his mobile to his mate.

'Charlie, we are on! I can't stop to talk now but I have the goods, mate. Meet me at my place at 10.30 this morning. See you then – and don't be late!'

He thought afterwards that he hadn't needed to mention being late, as Charlie was the most punctual guy he'd ever met.

Charlie was an old pal of Tim's. They had met when Tim was studying for his Computer Science degree and Charlie was doing Business Studies. It was at one of the students' social nights and at first they were very suspicious of each other but soon discovered they had a lot in common.

Whilst Tim had been lucky to find a job in computing almost immediately after he'd qualified, Charlie had been less successful and still had a temporary job as an attendant at a local petrol station working shifts – but at least it paid the bills.

Tim found that the lift in the flats was out of action again and, as he climbed the stairs to the fifth floor to his grubby one-bedroomed flat, he thought, as soon as I start coining it in, I shall be off, away from this dump.

Already he had hopes of buying his own place in a nicer part of the city. There was no way he could bring home any girlfriends to the flat as they'd have run a mile. Not that there were any girlfriends [or ever likely to be] on the scene, as Tim always gave them a wide berth.

His flat was now looking as tatty as ever, with wallpaper hanging off the walls, a pile of dishes in the cracked sink, discarded take-away containers, a strong smell of cabbage – and beer-stained carpets which stuck to your shoes.

He couldn't wait to unwrap the parcel and examine the contents, which were well packaged and labelled as computer hardware parts. He gave no thought to how the package had come through customs and assumed that there must be some agent in the UK working for the Far East manufacturer of the skimming devices. He carefully cut away the brown adhesive tape and there they were – three skimming devices, some very basic instructions written in both English and Chinese, with associated pin pads. He'd gone halves with Charlie on purchasing the devices and thought that this could be the best one and a half grand they had invested – and he hoped they would soon see a return on their investment.

The skimming devices were very crude, but he knew they would do the job. Tim had ordered one suitable for a normal card reader and two which could be slipped easily into ATMs with associated pin pads.

Just then there was a loud knock on the door and, heart thumping, he hurriedly hid the package under the old threadbare sofa, just in case. Losing his job with the police had made him very edgy and jumpy, to say the least.

'I'm coming! Be with you in a minute," he shouted, trying to have a quick tidy up on the way to the door.

He opened it gingerly.

'Christ, you're early, Charlie! You gave me a right fright,' he said. His heart was thumping.

'Come on, let's get on with it, Tim. Let's have a look at what we've bought. I'm as nervous about this as you are. I just hope we've got our money's worth.'

Tim went over to the sofa, recovered the package and opened up the first box.

'Take a look at this, then. Well, what do you think?' And he handed over the skimming device to Charlie.

'Bit basic isn't it? We don't seem to have much for our money! I just hope it works,' said Charlie, clearly disappointed.

'Think positive, Charlie! These will more than give us our money back in a matter of weeks. Now look, this is the one for the petrol station. You won't need a pin pad. I suggest we place it on the till that is used most frequently and leave it there for, say, a week, then lift it and move on elsewhere. We don't want to be too greedy in the same place, do we?'

'No, you're right, Tim. I'm on the night shift at the garage tonight and it's normally quiet about 10 o'clock so that should give me the time to slot it into one of the tills.' Charlie was beginning to show some excitement.

'Great! I'll do the same tonight at the Co-op ATM. The one inside the corner shop will have to wait – it's far too dodgy, as Tariq is away in India visiting his family and I don't want to risk that one. So are we all clear on what we are doing?'

'Yeah, it's no problem, Tim. Leave it to me. In excess of a thousand vehicles a week pass through so we should have a reasonable dump of data in a week's time.'

'Good. Ok. Well, let's go now. I have a twitter account to set up!'

Jean Price was an attractive, single twenty-five year old crime analyst who had been with the Midshire Police Force since leaving school. She'd progressed through the clerical side in the HR department and been selected by her manager to move into the analyst role. She had scored highly on the analyst assessment course and was a very competent young lady with a great deal of potential.

Jean arrived early for her first day. She parked down a side road and walked across to what looked like a pair of old semi-detached police houses and was about to ring the doorbell when a uniformed PC came out.

'I'm looking for DC Hodgson,' she said nervously.

'Oh, you'll find him and his team down the corridor in the end office,' said the PC, who didn't even question who she was and left the door open for her.

Jean thought that the security was rather lax: she hadn't even had to show her ID card. She walked down the dimly-lit corridor past boxes of A4 stationery which looked as though they had just arrived and found a door marked 'Operation Carousel.' She stepped into the Incident Room.

'Good morning. DI Harrison from MIT has sent me. Jean Price, your new analyst. Am I in the right place? I've been told to ask for DC Hodgson?'

'Good morning and welcome, Jean. Yes, you most certainly are in the right place. This is the Operation Carousel investigation room. I'm DC Jack Hodgson and this is my sidekick, DC Pete Bradley. Over there in the corner is Ted Wilson who is our indexer on the case.'

'Hello, Jean, nice to see you again,' said Ted, getting up to shake hands with her.

'Hi, Ted. Yes, it's been a long time! I didn't know you were working over here. This is a pleasant surprise! I thought you'd retired months ago.' Jean was now feeling less nervous.

'Yes, I did retire for a short period but, as they say, you can't keep a good man down! And to be honest I was starting to get underfoot at home! I think she-who-must-be-obeyed prefers me out of her way,' smirked Ted.

Ted was your typical retired copper: a heavily-built six footer. He had done his thirty years as a Police Constable but felt that, at the age of fifty, he still had something to offer the force, and so had come back, after just a few weeks of retirement, in a civilian position. He had a wealth of experience on case management as an indexer and researcher and had worked in many major incident rooms throughout the force.

'So, you two know each other then?' enquired DC Hodgson.

'Yes, we worked together on Operation Rosebowl,' said Jean. 'I'm looking forward to working with you again, Ted. We were a good team, you and I.'

'Likewise, Jean, likewise,' replied Ted, easing his large frame into his chair.

'Right, Jean, we have a briefing here in ten minutes, so your timing is perfect. It will save me time by not having to repeat myself. I suggest you have the desk next to Ted, then you can keep an eye on him and make sure he doesn't doze off!'

'Cheeky bugger, Hodgson! If anyone's going to nod off, it's you – particularly after you've had one of your lunch-time sessions,' was Ted Wilson's retort.

'DC Hodgson to you, Mr Wilson! Now, look, Ted – I've told you about those, they are what we call informal business meetings with some refreshments thrown in,' said DC Hodgson.

'Yeah, right! Sometimes the refreshments last a little bit longer than expected,' replied Ted.

'Sometimes the meetings last longer because we have a lot to discuss, Ted! As you can see, Jean, we have a bit of banter in this office, all healthy stuff for good team bonding! I'm sure you'll enjoy your time with us,' DC Hodgson laughed.

Just then DCI Bentley entered the room and boomed, 'Stand by your beds!' as he marched across the office.

'Good morning, sir. You took us by surprise again. I can see I am going to have to appoint a look-out in future,' said DC Hodgson jokingly as he stood to attention.

'Right, Hodgson! The element of surprise, my dear boy. Always surprise 'em – that's my motto. Now, look, I'm all ears, so what have you found so far? I need updating as soon as possible or the Detective Chief Superintendent will be having my guts for garters when he asks me how this is progressing at today's SIOs' meeting.'

DCI Bentley pulled up a chair.

'Well sir, it's early days, of course. As you know, it's only just been mentioned on Crimestoppers and there is nothing yet from that, of course, but I'm sure you appreciate, even at this early stage, there is certainly no shortage of data from what we got from the rental companies. In our specific area in the past eight weeks alone there have been in excess of four cases where hire cars have not been returned. And these are only vehicles which have been hired from various car rental companies in our area. There may be others of course that we don't know about.'

'What do you mean, in excess?' asked the DCI.

34

'Well, as I say sir, we believe there may be more. We think some haven't yet been reported missing.'

'Haven't been reported missing? But that's ridiculous! Don't they value their vehicle stock? What is the matter with these people! They've clearly got too much money.'

'Well, it appears that some of the car hire companies clearly don't want the publicity from the crimes, but as we've visited all the car hire companies in our area I am sure they will be reporting every incident to us from now on. Anyway, we're in the process of collating all the information we have with any past history of this type of crime and any previously known offenders. Jean here has joined us as our analyst on the team and she will be looking for any patterns or links within the data.'

'Excellent! It's nice to meet you Jean, and welcome to the team. I look forward to seeing what you come up with. So, do we have an operation name yet?'

'We do indeed, sir. We are working under the name of 'Operation Carousel.' Ted here came up with the name. Rather good I thought,' said DC Hodgson.

'Good God! Carousel! That takes me back to the days before the computer systems MICA, Autoindex and HOLMES, when all we had were carousel wheels of cards for investigations! How on earth we found anything in that card system amazed me. The amount of duplication in indexing cards was ridiculous. Can you imagine having to write seven different cards just to record one vehicle, for example? Do you know, in those days we even had to ask whether we could afford to ask the question of the card system. We had to decide which question we could ask and how much resource a question or line of enquiry would take before we did it. Anyway, I'm rambling on! Please do carry on, Hodgson.'

'Yes, sir. I'm glad to say technology has moved us on apace since those days.'

'You're right there, Hodgson, but it's moved the criminals on as well. That's the downside of course. We always have to keep one step ahead of them! Anyway, I'll leave you to get on with the tasks in hand. Let me know when you have something and we can arrange another meeting, but keep up the good work.' And the DCI left the room.

'Right, come on then, everyone! It's time for some hard graft. Pete, can you obtain full statements from each of the hire companies and I'll see if we can get office CCTV tapes from them. Ted, can you concentrate on indexing the data we have received so far, and Jean, can you get yourself up to speed with the data I loaded into XIM? It's going to be a steep learning curve but the sooner we get started on it, the better.'

CHAPTER 6

Wojek Kolowski had now picked up the keys for 27 Antrobus Street in Crewe, a delightful little three-bedroomed end terrace at the end of a cul-de-sac. He'd managed to knock the price down to £89,900 and was pleased with himself. It was a nice, quiet location – apart from the inter-city trains which thundered past at the end of the tiny but well-kept garden. With no house to sell and the property already vacant, everything had gone very smoothly for Wojek and far quicker than he had expected. The survey and all the paperwork had been completed on time. The bank had welcomed him as a new mortgage and current account customer and he was now firmly setup with a joint account. He also now had a shiny new credit card in his wallet together with a large bundle of £20 notes.

Yes, things were looking up for Wojek – and very soon a family of five were moving into their new home.

***

Jean Price had arrived in the office early the next morning and she was busy pulling together the many strands of data in Operation Carousel: data from car hire companies, insurance companies, missing vehicles, crime stoppers, vehicle sightings and so on – but, despite exploring all possible connections, there was no apparent link at this stage. Ted was also busy indexing the text from statements and as fast as these were being indexed DC Hodgson was raising more actions to obtain further information. This was going to be a long job but as a small incident team they all got on and worked well together.

'How are you getting on with the indexing?' asked DC Hodgson.

'Slow but sure,' replied Ted. 'I could do with some help on this.'

'I'll see what I can arrange,' said DC Hodgson. 'I'm not really sure why you need to index everything. Couldn't we rely on just text retrieval?'

'Well, we could, and of course we will use text retrieval searching to give us a safety net. But remember, even a safety net can have holes in it.'

'Yeah, ok, point taken,' replied DC Hodgson.

One of the recent actions raised by DC Hodgson was to obtain data from the ANPR (Automatic Number Plate Recognition) system of all the vehicle movement in the city area for the past ninety days. The IT department, after some resistance and only when DCI Bentley stepped in, duly provided an enormous dump of this data with thousands of records, and this was now sitting on one of the networked drives waiting to be processed.

'So, what's the next stage with this lot then, Jack? We don't even know what it is we are looking for! You can't be serious about importing all this into our case database, surely? We won't see the wood for the trees and we'll definitely drown in the data.'

DC Bradley scratched his head.

'Yes, I know Pete! My mistake. I hadn't realised the volume involved to be honest – but I do feel part of the answer has to be in this data somewhere. Any ideas, anyone?'

There was silence in the room. It reminded DC Hodgson of the time he'd worked on a major incident that didn't seem to be getting anywhere at all, with all leads coming to an abrupt end, and it had got so desperate that the SIO asked everyone to write down in an envelope who they thought did it! They were desperate times.

After what seemed like an endless silence Ted spoke up. 'Well, we do have the registrations of the stolen vehicles, don't we Jack – so that would be a start, wouldn't it?'

'But I'm still not sure what that actually gives us, Ted,' said DC Bradley.

'Well, it does give us the movement of the vehicles between various cameras of course,' said DC Hodgson. 'Jean, is it possible to filter this before we import it?'

'Yes, we can filter it and you're right, sir, this would really open the floodgates if we just import it as it stands at present. For starters I suggest we filter it, not just on the vehicle registrations that we know about, but also to include the relevant makes and models. You know, just the make and model of vehicles that have gone missing. I also suggest we keep it separate from our case database and use a temporary case file. That way, if we decide to drop this data, we haven't corrupted our main database. It shouldn't take me too long to import a filtered set and do an initial analysis using event charts. We'll at least get some sort of a timeline out of it,' replied Jean enthusiastically.

'Brilliant, Jean. Well, let's do that then, and see what it throws up. Ok everyone, back on your heads,' DC Hodgson cheerfully replied.

***

The petrol station on Highgate Road had been busy all day and Charlie Ellis, the shop attendant, was alone on the evening shift and getting more and more frustrated trying to find the right moment to slip the skimmer onto the card reader. Every time he thought it was the right moment, a customer would come in or the phone would go. All he needed was a couple of minutes, just two minutes that's all. In his head he'd rehearsed the move; he'd gone over it several times, memorising the instructions. Finally, at 10.15pm, his moment came. It was quiet, no one was in sight. He pretended to tidy up the counter. Ideally he would have switched off the CCTV in the corner of the shop, but it was alarmed. So, as discreetly as possible, he re-stacked the sweets and special offers at the side of the counter and moved the notice advertising the £4.99 special offer garden solar lights so as to avoid the CCTV view. With a swift move, covering his hand, he slotted in the skimming device. That was easier than I expected, he thought, and minutes later a customer drove onto the forecourt in a black BMW Series 5 and started filling up with diesel. That was close, but would it work, he thought. What if it throws up an error, what if it jams and I have to call out the manager?

But it was too late now for what ifs and five minutes later the shop door opened.

'Pump 1, please and a packet of Marlboro Lights,' said the customer, pulling the credit card from his wallet.

'Certainly, sir, that will be £65.10. Would you like a vat receipt?'

'No thanks,' said the customer, sliding his credit card into the reader and tapping in his pin number.

40

Charlie watched patiently as the connection processed the card.

'Great, that's fine – you can remove your card now,' said Charlie, handing over the receipt, finally relieved that the card reader was still functioning as normal.

'Have a nice day.'

Have a nice day he thought, and it's 10.20 at night! There's not much of it left!

'One down, many to go,' he said to himself, rubbing his hands as the customer drove off.

***

'Do you fancy another pint, Jack? Just one for the road,' said Pete, who had already signalled to the barman to bring over two pints.

'Well, all right, just one more, but I must get back to the office soon before the DCI calls in. Rumour has it he's likely to drop into the office this afternoon,' replied DC Hodgson.

'Do you know, it's a strange one this, Pete. I've been up all night racking my brains on the scam that's going on here. You think about it, a man – well at least we think it's a man – hires a car for two days. He pays up front in cash – in fact I didn't even know some car hire companies would take cash – he has all the right paperwork, drives off, and he and the car are never seen again. Then the same thing happens a few weeks later. Someone somewhere must have their suspicions.'

'Do you think the cars could be on the continent by now?' replies Pete, taking the top off his fresh pint of bitter and handing over a tenner to the barman.

'No, I don't think so. It's possible, of course, but I have a feeling the cars are still in this country.'

Just then the door burst open and Jean Price rushed in.

'Sorry to trouble you, sir. Ted said I'd find you here. Can we have a chat? I think I'm onto something,' she said excitedly.

'Yes, yes, keep your voice down, Jean! Look, I keep telling you, you can call me Jack.'

'Right, sorry sir, I mean, Jack! I did what we agreed and I imported a filtered set of ANPR data using a number of filters. It took a while but I eventually ended up with a database of vehicle details, registrations, dates, times, locations, direction of travel and so on. I connected our Link Analysis software to the data and set it looking for common links.'

'Don't tell me it found some!'

'Well, no, not exactly,' replied Jean, 'but what I did next was to widen the import locations, but instead of concentrating on the Manchester area, I widened it out to the M6 Junction 18 including up to Junction 23 Haydock and then did a further import. I was working on the basis that they could be using the motorway to move out of our area. I was planning to widen it further to include the M62 East and West but there was no need. I have found two vehicles which are certainly of interest to us.'

'So what is so different about these two vehicles and why do they stand out in particular?' asked DC Hodgson.

'It's not what's different about them sir, sorry, I mean Jack, it's what is identical with them – believe it or not they both have the same vehicle registration plate, and were twenty-six miles apart at exactly the same time and date!' said Jean excitedly.

'Impossible! The same number plate? It can't be! Have you checked the ANPR system for the date and time? The cameras are probably not set up correctly,' said DC Bradley.

'Yes, I did that with our IT department and double checked it. The ANPR clock is synchronised across all the cameras and in this data we have a vehicle sighted at Holmes Chapel and one identically clocked at Haydock over twenty miles away at the same time and travelling in opposite directions.'

'I still don't believe this. It could only happen if you were driving the Tardis!' said DC Bradley, chuckling to himself and taking another swig from his pint.

'Well, it's true Pete, I assure you. I've checked everything.'

'This could be the breakthrough, Pete, we were after,' said DC Hodgson, getting up and leaving what was left of his pint. 'Get your coat on! Well done, Jean – good work. Can you get me both images from those ANPR cameras? Come on now, drink up and let's get back to the office quick and do a PNC check on the vehicle.'

'I can't rush my beer Jack – it'll give me wind, and I assure you, yer wouldn't want that! I'll follow you down there,' replied Pete.

CHAPTER 7

Tim slept in that morning. He'd had a late night working in the Jelly Bean café on a piece of source code that had to be finished and he was eventually asked to leave at one o'clock by Alan, the café owner, who was tired of waiting and wanted to lock up.

Tim had a good relationship with Alan. They had met in the pub a few weeks earlier and since then he had helped Alan out a number of times with removal of viruses and Trojans that, despite anti-virus software, somehow regularly appear on the workstations in the internet café.

Tim had continued working on the source code on his laptop at home, something he was trying to avoid in case he was being monitored but he had no option under the circumstances. After his dismissal he didn't trust the police and he had started to get a phobia about being followed everywhere.

It was 11.30am when he finally arose from his bed. He had a quick cold water lick in the bathroom and grabbed a piece of toast and cup of tea before heading back to the café. He knew he would have to get in there before the students arrived at lunchtime from the nearby university and took over every internet connection.

Once inside the café he ordered a black coffee which he needed just to stay awake. He logged on, plugged in his USB memory stick and setup the new twitter account. That was the easy bit.

Next he downloaded his source code to the targeted web address and sent out the social media connection invite request. As soon as his target connected with the invite he would have everything he needed, username and password. It was now a case of waiting for stage one to take place. He didn't have to wait long.

***

DC Pete Bradley was now back in the Operation Carousel office. He logged onto PNC and brought up the details of the car registration on his computer screen.

'It's a company car, red Ford Mondeo Titanium X 2.2 TDCI, registered last year, belonging to Northern Computer Systems based in Congleton, Cheshire,' he shouted across the office.

'Nice motor, Pete. Right, well that should be easy to follow up. It's only down the A34 so get your coat on and let's get down there straight away and find out who the company car driver is,' said DC Hodgson.

'No sooner said than done! Ted, can you drive us down to Congleton? Jack and I have had a beer or two so we daren't risk it. We'll hopefully be back later this afternoon, Jean.'

'I wouldn't bank on it,' said DC Hodgson, grabbing his jacket.

And they left the office.

Within forty-five minutes Ted was driving the unmarked police car through the leafy lanes of Cheshire.

'It's nice around here, isn't it?' said Ted. 'I wouldn't mind living here when I eventually seriously retire.'

'You've got no chance, Ted, on your police pension – unless you have a lottery win! These properties are serious money, mate. This is professional footballers' territory and a stock broker belt,' said Pete.

'Yeah, I know – but you can dream, can't you! Now, where on earth is this turning we are supposed to be looking for?'

By now they were convinced they were lost. There was nothing but stables and farms, then suddenly they came across a quite impressive, ivy-clad building which was set back in landscaped grounds with its own security gates. There was a large notice on the gate; 'Keep Out – Beware of Guard Dogs. You have been warned.' They pressed the intercom and a voice came back, 'Northern Computer Systems. Can I help you, do you have an appointment?'

'Midshire Police – and no, we don't have an appointment! Officers DC Hodgson and DC Bradley. Can you let us in, please?' said DC Hodgson.

The electric gates swung open at a painfully slow pace and they drove in down a sweeping gravel driveway and parked up in front of the building.

'This is a bit impressive, Ted. You stay in the car. We shouldn't be long in here,' said DC Hodgson.

'Don't worry, Jack, I'm going nowhere – particularly if there are guard dogs roaming around here somewhere,' replied Ted.

They made their way across the gravel path to the imposing front door which had already been opened for them. They strolled through to reception where they were met by a smartly-dressed young lady. 'Good afternoon officers, welcome to Northern Computer Systems. My name is Jane Birkshaw and I'm the Operations Director here. Now, how can we help you?'

DC Hodgson flashed his warrant card and showed her an image from the ANPR system. 'Good afternoon Miss. We are investigating a number of incidents and we need to trace the driver of this vehicle, a red Ford Mondeo, JX12YUV. We believe it to be registered to your company. Is that correct?'

The young lady retrieved a folder from behind the reception desk and glanced down a list of vehicles.

'Yes, that is one of ours. It is assigned to Mike Johnson in our Sales Department.'

'Can you please provide us with an address for Mr Johnson? I assume he doesn't work here?' DC Bradley prepared to jot down the details.

'Yes, we can certainly provide you with his address. Mike is based in our Northampton office and his home address is, let me see now, yes here it is – 43 Westbourne Avenue, Milton Keynes. I'm afraid I don't have a postcode though.'

'That will be fine, Miss – we don't need a postcode,' replied DC Hodgson.

'Tell me, does anyone else have access to this vehicle? Could anyone else have been driving this car at that time?' enquired DC Bradley.

'Sorry, at what time?'

'Last Thursday, the 17th October, at around 4pm.'

'Well, all employees are insured to drive all company cars – but you'd have to ask Mike whether he had handed the car keys over to anyone on that particular day. Um… is there anything we should know about this? Is Mike in some sort of trouble?' enquired Jane anxiously.

'I'm afraid there is nothing we can tell you at this point and I would appreciate it if you don't mention to Mr Johnson or, for that matter anyone else in the company, that we have been enquiring about his vehicle.

But thank you, you have been most helpful. Goodbye for now.'

'I quite understand. Goodbye,' replied Jane as she closed the heavy oak door behind them.

'Do you fancy a trip down to Milton Keynes then, Pete?' said DC Hodgson as they sped out of the driveway.

'Too right I do! There's some nice pubs down there! When?'

'Now, of course! Let's strike while the iron is hot, Ted! Head for the M6 southbound, and set the sat nav for Milton Keynes. We have a Mr Johnson to visit this evening. It's going to be a long day, I'm afraid.'

CHAPTER 8

Alan Jackson was sitting at home watching Coronation Street when his home laptop bleeped with a new email message. He'd had a long, hard day at Police HQ with two of the five Divisional Crime Recording servers going down and the Police and Crime Commissioner (PCC) onto him to find out what progress there was on the force mobile app development. His team had worked their socks off to get both servers fixed and when they were finally up and running and he was about to leave at around five o'clock the PCC himself rang to congratulate him on restoring the service so efficiently. Yes, Alan Jackson had driven home in a happy mood that day. He was tired but pleased with himself. He ran a tight ship and efficiency was his thing.

Divorced twice, he now lived by himself in a modest semi-detached house in Cheadle and he was never happier than when he was either at work or gardening. He'd been in the police force for twenty-two years and had been moved into the IT department as a young inspector five years earlier. He'd had rapid promotion to Superintendent and was well-respected throughout the force.

Normally Alan wouldn't think about opening any emails in the evening and right now all he wanted to do was relax, put his feet up and watch the telly. However, on this occasion he opened the email which was an invite by the PCC himself to connect with him on the business link social media site. Before he had had time to think about it, he had clicked on the link, typed in his username and password and accepted the invite.

He settled back into his armchair to watch a documentary on motor caravanning, another one of his passions, and very soon he'd dropped off to sleep.

Whilst he slept the silent download had already been activated.

***

'This must be the place. It's a bit posh,' said Ted as they drove into the exclusive housing estate. 'Number forty-three – there it is, in the corner. And the Mondeo's in the driveway so it looks as if he's at home and we haven't had a wasted journey.'

'OK, Ted, you park up here and have a well-earned rest and Pete and I will go in and interview our Mr Johnson. I'm looking forward to this,' said DC Hodgson.

'Take your time, boss. I'm going to get some shut-eye,' said Ted as he fully reclined the driver's seat.

DC Hodgson and DC Bradley strolled up to the house and rang the doorbell. Minutes later, after the dog inside had finally stopped barking, an attractive red head answered the door and waited for one of them to speak.

'Hello! Mrs Johnson, we presume? I'm Detective Constable Hodgson and this is Detective Constable Bradley. We are sorry to trouble you, but is your husband at home this evening?'

'Yes, he is. Can I ask what this is about?' She seemed somewhat apprehensive.

'There is nothing to concern you, Mrs Johnson. We'd just like to have a few words with your husband,' replied DC Hodgson.

'Yes, certainly, officer. I'll tell him you are here,' and she turned and shouted down the hallway. 'Darling, it's for you! There are two police officers wishing to see you.'

They waited at the front door in the darkness until Mike Johnson, dressed in jeans, tee shirt and trainers, appeared in the hallway.

'Can I help you? What on earth has happened? It's not my mother, is it?' he asked anxiously.

DC Bradley thought twice about saying, 'Do I look like your mother?' but thought better of it.

'No, sir, it's not your mother, but we would like you to answer a few questions for us,' said DC Hodgson.

'Yes, of course, please come in.'

They followed the Johnsons down the hallway and into the lounge, waited for them to sit down and then sat in the two remaining armchairs.

'Are you Mike Johnson who works for Northern Computer Systems and the driver of the company car a Ford Mondeo JX12YUV?' asked DC Bradley, looking at his notes.

'Yes, I am and you have just passed the car in the driveway.'

DC Bradley thought, 'Smart-arse!' and felt a bit foolish at this point.

'Well, would you mind telling us where you were on October 17th at approximately 4pm?' asked DC Hodgson.

'Let me think now.' Mike Johnson rubbed his chin. 'Yes, that was a week ago, it was a Thursday, I had gone up to Head Office in Cheshire for one of our sales meetings and probably around that time I would be heading home, say around the Holmes Chapel area on the M6 southbound.'

He paused. 'Now, look, what is this all about? Have I been speeding or something?'

'No, not as far as we are aware, sir,' said DC Hodgson. 'Would you also have been in the Haydock area in that same afternoon?'

'No, of course not. My sales patch is East Anglia. I don't even know where Haydock is. It's a race course, isn't it? Now, won't you please tell me what this is all about?'

'Was there anyone travelling with you in the car?' asked DC Hodgson.

'Yes, I had my sales manager with me.'

'And his name, sir, would be?'

'Arthur Fellows. He was with me all day.'

DC Hodgson continued to make notes and thought about further questions but decided to leave it at that for the time being.

'Now, officer, can you please tell us what is this all about? What on earth has my husband done wrong?' asked Mrs Johnson.

'That is what we are trying to ascertain, Mrs Johnson. Well, that will be all for now. We may need to come back and have a further meeting but thank you for your time. We'll let ourselves out. Thanks for your cooperation, Mr Johnson.'

DC Hodgson and DC Bradley were now in the hallway and as they shut the front door behind them they could hear Mike Johnson having the third degree from his wife.

'Do you reckon he's telling the truth?' said DC Bradley.

'Oh, yes, no problem there,' came the reply.

'The plot thickens!' said DC Bradley, getting into the car.

'It does, Pete. We are no further on. Come on, I need a pint! Ted, find us a nice little tavern somewhere and then we'll head up t'north,' said DC Hodgson gloomily.

CHAPTER 9

Tim Ridgway had agreed to meet Charlie at Tim's flat after his afternoon shift at the petrol station.

He was now at home watching 'Goggle Box,' one of his favourite programmes, when the alert email came through on his mobile. All it said was, '*Stage One complete.*'

Great, thought Tim, now rubbing his hands. I can now start planning for the next stage.

As he was thinking things through, the doorbell went and it was Charlie, who was as punctual as ever.

'Hi Charlie, have you got everything?' said Tim anxiously. 'You didn't get spotted did you?'

'Sure have, Tim – and no, I was very careful. I've retrieved the skimmer and believe it or not we have a dump of some two hundred credit and debit card details,' said Charlie excitedly.

'I thought there would have been more,' said Tim, clearly somewhat disappointed.

'Well, no. We ran it for a week as agreed and of course there are five tills at the garage and we've only had it on the first till. Remember we said we wouldn't be greedy. I mean two hundred will keep us busy – and we can sell on some of them if needed,' remarked Charlie.

'I've been thinking, Charlie. I know we said we wouldn't be greedy but I wonder whether installing the skimmer in the pay-at-the-pump would be easier?' Tim looked thoughtful.

'How do you mean, Tim?'

'Well, it would need some modification, which I think I could do,' said Tim. 'In the past, most skimming has taken place at ATMs, where we can mask the real card slot with our own device which of course is disguised to look like the real thing. But what if we could say, actually insert the device inside the pump. To trap those customers who use it at night or prefer to pay at the pump with their card. You know, the ones who pay at the pump instead of at the kiosk. The device would be well hidden inside the pump and no one would ever know, would they?'

'That's bloody brilliant, Tim! Well, I suppose it could work. Of course not everyone uses the pay at the pump, I think they'd prefer to come into the shop and I'd need time to work out how on earth we could install it without being spotted. Let me think about that and get back to you. Anyway, how did you get on? Did you retrieve the ATM skimmer?' enquired Charlie.

'Well, the ATM wasn't as busy as I thought. I've recovered everything – the skimmer and pin pad, and we have a dump of about fifty cards. I don't know about you, but I think we'll lie low for now with these. I have enough on my plate at present,' said Tim.

'Yeah, I'm sorry to hear about you losing your job, Tim.'

'Aw, they did me a favour, Charlie. I was getting so bloody fed up in that office, I needed to move on. To be honest I'd passed my sell-buy date there. I was stagnating. Do you know it had got to the point where I hated going into the place and I think they knew it. I'm better off out of there.'

'Still, I'm sure you'll soon get another job. Are you going on Jobseekers' allowance?'

'Well, I might do – be worth picking up a few extra quid.'

'So, presumably you'll start looking soon for another IT job?'

'Yeah, possibly. Look, I'm not sure I even want another job. Let's see how this little project goes. If it goes well I might not need another job. Anyway, back to these. I suggest you take for now, say, details for ten cards and I'll do the same. Tariq is back tomorrow and he can create the cloned cards for us. Use them carefully, of course! We don't want to rush things. And above all, don't make it obvious!' said Tim.

'Right,' said Charlie. 'I have no plans to drive up in a Roller just yet!'

CHAPTER 10

Jean Price was still analysing the ANPR data in the incident room when DC Hodgson and DC Bradley arrived back from their trip down south. They seemed somewhat exhausted after their journey.

'How did you get on yesterday, Jack?' she enquired

'It was very tiring Jean, as you can imagine, it was a long day and, to be honest, not as well as I expected,' said DC Hodgson, 'but I've been thinking, we do need to identify the routes of these vehicles. Remember we do have the stolen vehicle registrations, well, I think surely we should be able to track the movements of these in the city.'

'Well, that's true to a degree, Jack, but the ANPR camera locations are not everywhere in the city you know, with the right knowledge of where they are located you could of course drive in and avoid every camera, and to be honest the cars could have been driven straight out of our area,' said DC Bradley.

'No, Pete, I appreciate that, but there are also CCTV cameras positioned throughout the city and using a combination of event data and a manual CCTV recordings check we might just be able to plot the route,' said Jean.

'Exactly, Jean, that's a lot of manual work and it's a long shot but it could be worth it,' said DC Hodgson thoughtfully. 'Look, I suggest we tackle this as follows.

Jean, can you produce a timeline for each stolen vehicle that is picked up on each ANPR location and then pass the charts to Ted. Ted, for each of these charts can you then identify further possible camera locations, you should then be able to get a list of these from the main Command and Control room. When we have these we can obtain the CCTV recordings for those times and manually look for the car registrations in question.'

'You are not serious, are you, Jack? That'll take us ages to manually view those and some of them are in different video formats, some are even very poor image quality,' said Pete.

'Deadly serious, Pete, I think it's our best shot at present, in the meantime you and me are off to see if we can enhance those images of Mike Johnson's car.'

***

Tim Ridgway was now the owner of ten cloned credit/debit cards, having got Tariq to create the clones. He'd already used seven of them by touring a number of ATMs in various surrounding areas over a period of days and pocketed about £20k in total. The plan was to ditch them after a couple of weeks and move onto another set of cards.

He had already bought four laptops online using the card details, one for himself and three to sell on for cash at a cut-down price to some of the students in the cafe. He had taken the opportunity to chat to a number of them in the Jelly Bean café. The Citroen AX had now been part-exchanged for a nifty VW Golf paid for in cash. He was disappointed, however, when he went to pick the Golf up from the used car dealer, to see his old Citroen being loaded onto the back of a truck destined for the crusher at the scrap yard.

Although Charlie and he had agreed not to use the cards immediately or be greedy he'd found it far too tempting by being able to buy anything he wanted, when he wanted. He caved in to this temptation and treated himself to a wardrobe of new clothes from a number of shops in the Arndale Centre.

He was now planning his next move and decided that it was about time that he launched stage two of his revenge plan. Whilst he was at home he carefully disassembled one of the gonks he had previously retrieved from various computer terminals including the Crime section at Midshire Police. He disconnected the memory card from the tiny camera buried in the Gonk and then plugged the card into his laptop and examined the files. As expected, sure enough there they were, images of usernames and passwords could clearly be seen being entered on the force keyboards. He now had everything he needed for the next part of his plan; he went back to the Jelly Bean café, ordered himself a coffee and took a seat in the corner. Alan, the café owner, couldn't get over how Tim had smartened himself up virtually overnight; the hoodie was still present but the new jeans and trainers stood out like a sore thumb. Soon he was connected to the Crimestoppers online form portal, but via the backdoor he had previously setup for himself, and he was now into the administrators' area. He copied the carefully worded text he had prepared, saved it several times, updated the audit trail and ran the code he had uploaded. On completion he smiled to himself as he closed down the connection to the server.

CHAPTER 11

Every month the Midshire Police analyst group met to discuss issues that were affecting them. They covered everything including crime trends, projects, tips, techniques, problem software, etc. but in truth it was a great opportunity to catch up with friends, have a good natter, and put the world to rights and get together afterwards for a glass or two of wine.

This month Jean had managed to get some time off from the Operation Carousel investigation to attend the meeting, which was always held in the Principal Analysts office in Force HQ at 3pm on the last Wednesday of the month.

'Welcome, everyone, and may I say what a good turn out this month,' said Barbara Smith, the principal analyst. 'We have a lot to get through this afternoon so let's start with you, Jane Can you tell us what have you been working on since we last met, in complete confidence of course?'

'Well, hmm, I've recently transferred to working with the Major Incident team at present, working on the murder incident down at Wilmslow on the Holmes system, I should be there for the next three months, we are now preparing the case data for court,' said Jane Ellis, somewhat nervously.

'And you, Fiona, which projects are you working on at present?' asked Barbara as she made notes for the minutes.

'Good afternoon, everyone, I'm working at PSD on a force misconduct case and, much as I would like to tell you about it, I'm afraid it is sensitive so I can't say more than that,' replied Fiona.

'We quite understand, Fiona, and you, Richard?'

'Good afternoon, yes I'm also back at MIT working on Operation Trident doing credit and debit card fraud analysis. You may or may not be aware that there has been a marked increase in this type of crime in the force area and it looks like I could be on this for quite some time. In fact the volumes are such that I will probably be requiring quite a bit of help soon,' said Richard confidently.

'Thank you, Richard. I gather you are also going to give us a presentation in a moment on this trend we are encountering, and how the thieves are using these so called skimming devices and committing card fraud. Just let me know if we can help in any way. And now you, Jean, I gather you have just been seconded to Operation Carousel. This is a new investigation, I understand, and I'm curious to hear what this actually covers, perhaps you can update us on your project.'

'Yes, that's right, Barbara, I'd just finished on the Morrison murder case, which as you probably know is awaiting a court date at present, and I'm currently working on Operation Carousel with DC Hodgson and DC Bradley on a complex stolen vehicle investigation. It's early days yet but it looks as though I could be on this for quite a few months. We are talking multiple vehicles here, where people are hiring cars and not returning them. We believe the vehicles are being stolen

61

to order, sold on in other parts of the country or maybe even delivered abroad.'

'Thank you, Jean, that investigation sounds most interesting and I'm sure you will be actively involved in assisting the team on that. Now, Richard, back to you, the floor is now yours. Tell us what we need to know about trends in card fraud and how we may be able to help,' said Barbara, handing over the presentation laptop.

'Thanks, Barbara, well, where do I start? I know some of you will already be aware of this type of crime, so please forgive me if I'm going over old ground. I have a number of PowerPoint slides here which illustrate the problem.'

Richard stood up, switched his laptop on and started his presentation display.

'Firstly, what is skimming? Well, effectively it is a term used to describe a method of removing bank information from either debit or credit cards. The thieves don't really care what type of card they steal details from. Little did people realise when the first plastic credit card came into circulation in the 1950s how skimming devices could be made to extract the bank information held within it. Sixty years ago, skimming might have referred to, say, stealing money from an employer's payroll, but in the current world thieves use all sorts of methods to skim data from cards. So what does a skimming device look like? Well, it will usually incorporate two components; a magnetic card reader to capture the bank details and possibly a small camera to capture the keying details on the keypad. The thief then uses this captured data to copy or clone the card.'

'But how do would-be thieves install or remove this equipment without being seen?' asked Barbara.

'Well, you think about it, whenever you go to an ATM to withdraw cash you always guard your details being entered, or at least you should do. Well, thieves only need a short time to install or even remove the devices and presumably guard themselves to make sure no one sees what they are in fact doing. They usually choose a time, say early in the morning or late at night, when no one is about,' replied Richard.

'But it's not only ATMs which are being modified by thieves; we have seen a spate of incidents where petrol stations are being targeted. Just consider this. Pretty much everybody filling up with petrol uses some form of credit or debit card to pay for it and recently we've seen an increase in the force area of this type of crime.'

'A lot of people assume their details have been stolen through online purchasing, you know through malware or spy software, but it appears most of it happens through skimmers.'

'But where do they get these skimming devices from?' asked Jean.

'They typically buy them online via the dark web, they vary from being a really cheap plastic affair to quite sophisticated devices. We believe some of the plastic devices can now even be printed on 3D printers.'

'But presumably chip and pin has helped in keeping the number of fraud cases down?' asked Fiona.

'Well, yes, it has helped to a degree, but the fraudsters, through various means, also embed micro cameras that can capture the pin number as well. Believe it or not some of the devices can be incorporated in a complete replacement cover which fits over the ATM itself.'

The meeting continued discussing the issues with card fraud, the current data imports and the plans for the next analysts' refresher training course, but it was quite apparent that the likely workload for the foreseeable future would be from stolen vehicles and card fraud.

***

Superintendent Jackson was chairing an internal meeting to discuss the implementation plan of the new Command and Control System. With the installation just 12 months away this was going to be a very busy time for the IT department. They were just going through the project Gantt chart discussing each implementation stage when Superintendent Jackson's secretary, Samantha Newing, came bursting in.

'I'm very sorry to interrupt, Sir, but Chief Inspector Newton from PSD is in your office and would like to see you for five minutes,' said Samantha, holding the door ajar.

'Can't it wait, Samantha? I really am very busy here, we have a lot to get through. If it's about that Ridgway incident, tell him I have completed all the paperwork for the HR department and I posted it in the internal post last night,' said Superintendent Jackson impatiently.

'He didn't say what it was about, Superintendent, all he would say is that it is quite urgent, he really seemed quite desperate to speak with you,' replied Samantha.

'Oh very well, tell him I'll be there in two minutes,' said Superintendent Jackson irritably.

'Very well Superintendent, I'll send him into your office,' replied Samantha, closing the door behind her.

'You'll have to carry on without me for a short while gentlemen, I am very sorry about this, hopefully this won't take too long and I'll be back to continue our discussion,' said Superintendent Jackson to the staff gathered round the conference table as he got up and left.

Superintendent Jackson made his way down the corridor to his office, where Chief Inspector Newton was sitting waiting patiently.

'Now, what is all this about, Chief Inspector, couldn't this wait for another time? I am in the middle of a very important planning meeting,' said Superintendent Jackson.

'No, I'm sorry to drag you away from your meeting, Superintendent, and I'm afraid it couldn't wait, I have a somewhat delicate matter that I need to discuss with you rather urgently,' replied Chief Inspector Newton.

'Well, what is it?' said Superintendent Jackson, somewhat impatiently.

'Well, Superintendent, I'm not sure where to start on this,' said Chief Inspector Newton hesitatingly

'Well, why not try at the beginning?' snapped Superintendent Jackson. 'I don't have a lot of spare time you know today.'

'Well sir, it appears that Crimestoppers have received a number of anonymous messages from a number of locations regarding yourself. Some of these messages are from outside the force area and some are even from as far away as overseas,' said Chief Inspector Newton, thinking carefully on choosing his words and now pausing.

'And, well, go on?' said Superintendent Jackson impatiently

'And they all relate to this, that allegedly you have been selling pornographic material to a number of people online,' replied the Chief Inspector.

'What! Don't be ridiculous, that's preposterous, I have never heard such rubbish in all my life, the Crimestoppers portal has been hacked surely. I'll look into it as soon as my meeting this morning is over, we have an audit log which should pick this sort of thing up.

Now, if you don't mind I have a very busy schedule and I really must get on,' said Superintendent Jackson, getting his diary out.

'Well, I agree Superintendent, but it's not as easy as that, I'm afraid. I'm sure you understand we have to investigate every one of these claims,' said the Chief Inspector.

'Yes, of course I do, completely. So may I ask how you plan to investigate these ridiculous claims?'

'Well, I'm afraid we will have to collect your force laptop and any PC equipment you have at home in the first instance, I assume we have your full cooperation?'

'But of course you do, I will bring my home laptop in tomorrow, my force laptop is on my desk over there. I have nothing to hide, I assure you, you can take that now. Now, if that's all, I really must get on.'

'Sorry, sir, but that won't do I'm afraid, we will need to accompany you to your home right now to obtain the laptop.'

'Right now! Damn it, man, I'm in the middle of a very important planning meeting,' stormed Superintendent Jackson.

'Sir, I am afraid we do have to treat this with some urgency,' replied Chief Inspector Newton.

'Very well, but let's get on with it,' sighed Superintendent Jackson, handing over his force laptop.

'Our plan sir, is to send both laptops to our Hi-Tech Crime unit for examination, I'm sure we can return them to you as soon as possible,' said Chief Inspector Newton, pleased that at least the initial meeting was over.

'Come on, then, let's get on with it, the sooner we get this over with the better,' said Superintendent Jackson, getting up and opening the door.

***

DC Hodgson and DC Bradley were studying the enhanced images in the ANPR support office.

'Can you zoom in a little bit further, Pete?' said Jack, leaning into the screen.

'That's just about on the limit now,' replied Pete, 'it is as good as it gets, I'm afraid.'

'Well, the date is right, the time is right and you can clearly see there is definitely only one person travelling in the Ford Mondeo going northbound on the M6 motorway at Haydock and you can see he has a beard and is wearing glasses. The image from Holmes Chapel also confirms Mike Johnson's story, you can see the Ford Mondeo, same registration, this time going southbound. There is an elderly man sitting in the passenger seat next to him, who I guess is Arthur Fellows, his manager, but there's no doubt about it, it's the same vehicle,' said DC Bradley.

'Not exactly, Pete, it's the same make, model and colour etc. but with the same number plate,' replied DC Hodgson. 'Do you know, I think we have a cloned vehicle fraud on our hands here, we have a situation where we have two identical cars, carrying the same number plate, being driven around the UK at the same time, and from a police perspective the vehicle is insured and taxed.'

'The question is how on earth can we trace the driver of the second vehicle?' asked DC Bradley.

'Well, it's quite possible, of course, that the driver that is going northbound is in fact the thief.'

'Or the driver of the second vehicle is driving around as an innocent party in all this, having bought the car, which is already taxed, in good faith. I would go as far as saying that the second driver probably doesn't even know he is driving a cloned car and thinks he is in fact the new owner,' suggested DC Hodgson.

'Are you sure, Jack?'

'Well, no, I'm not sure but I'd place a wager on it, shall we say a fiver?' said DC Hodgson, stretching out his hand.

'You know I am not a betting man, Jack,' replied DC Bradley.

'Well, come on then, Pete, let's go and see how Jean and Ted are getting on with identifying the possible routes of all the stolen vehicles.'

CHAPTER 12

*The Arndale Centre was busier than normal on that
Saturday morning, it was half-term and it was bustling
with shoppers who were getting ready for the
forthcoming holiday season.*

*The dark haired lady had been on a spending spree
accompanied by her three children, she was now loading
up her shopping in the back of the Volvo estate in the
multi-storey car park. The children were now getting
rather impatient and wanted to know when they could go
for lunch to their favourite fast food restaurant.*

*They had been to what felt like every clothes shop in
the shopping mall and were now loaded up with leisure
wear, swimwear, shoes, trainers etc. in readiness for
their family holiday two week summer break.*

*In a few weeks' time they would be flying off to the
sun from Manchester Airport to Tenerife.*

CHAPTER 13

Detective Sergeant Webster, as DC Hodgson's team leader, decided it was about time he visited the Operation Carousel investigation to see how they were progressing. Since the government cutbacks the force had reduced the staff drastically in all departments, resulting in an emergency force reorganisation. DS Webster had picked up a number of teams that he was now responsible for and he spent most of his time these days supervising small investigation teams rather than being part of a bigger team. He parked up in a side street and made his way down the steps to the converted semi-detached house in Cheadle. The house, which was originally part of the old police training college known as Broomfields, had seen better days, but it was ideal for an investigation team away from the disturbances of divisional HQ.

He rang the doorbell and a charming, attractive young lady, who was working in the Crime Statistics unit in the property, opened the door.

'Can I help you?' she said.

'Yes, I'm Detective Sergeant Webster, visiting DC Hodgson,' said DS Webster, showing his warrant card and at the same time admiring her shapely figure.

'Oh, right, yes sir, they are in the back room just down the hallway on the right.'

'I wouldn't mind getting you in the back room,' thought DS Webster.

'Thank you very much, I'll find my way down there,' said DS Webster, who had already set off down the corridor at a fast pace.

DS Webster pushed open the door, which was signed Operation Carousel, and was confronted with a stack of cardboard boxes piled high, he could just about see over the top.

'Hello, is there anyone in here?' he enquired.

'Oh, hello Sarge, come in if you can, we were expecting you but I'm afraid we didn't have time to move things around,' said DC Bradley.

DS Webster managed to squeeze past all the boxes. 'What on earth is this lot?'

'CCTV recordings sir, as you can see we are inundated with them, but we are making progress, albeit slowly,' said DC Bradley.

'Ah, good morning, Sarge, welcome to our operation room. I'd give that 20 minutes,' said DC Hodgson, wafting his hand to Ted as he returned from the toilet.

'Good morning, Jack, I see you have soon settled in here, and perhaps you'd introduce me to everyone?' said DS Webster.

'Yes, certainly, Sarge. Now everyone, listen up, this is DS Webster from Divisional HQ, DC Bradley who you know, Ted Wilson who I think you remember from the Whitley case and this is Jean Price, our new analyst on the team.'

'Good morning, everyone. Perhaps you can give me a quick appraisal of where we are at present, naturally I have read your interim report, Jack, but it would be good to hear it from the horse's mouth, so to speak, just in case the DCI asks me my opinion,' said DS Webster, taking a seat at the conference table in the centre of the room.

DC Hodgson wheeled across a large notice board which contained a number of photographs and maps.

'Yes certainly, Sarge. Well, we are making some progress, albeit much slower than we would like. I think very soon we will have identified where these stolen vehicles are being garaged, this is our priority at present. As you know, Sarge, we have a situation at present where we believe there are in fact duplicate vehicles being driven around the country. Of course we could be wrong, and maybe the vehicles are in fact being exported, but the identification of the two identical red Ford Mondeos being driven on the M6 at the same time in opposite directions leads us to believe that the cars are in fact being re-plated. So the plan for the time being is to concentrate on that particular registration, which we think will lead us to the person or gang that's behind these thefts,' said DC Hodgson.

'So, let me get this straight, I'm driving around in my patrol car with built in ANPR, the car in front of me is one of the stolen ones which has had its registration plates changed and, assuming the vehicle carrying the new number plate has been taxed and insured, we wouldn't even be alerted and wouldn't even know anything was amiss?' said DS Webster.

'Bang on, Sarge, that's exactly what we believe is happening,' replied DS Hodgson.

'Well, they must be selling these privately, surely they wouldn't risk car auctions or main dealers, and what about the registration documents of the vehicle?' said DS Webster.

'Well, we don't know, Sarge, they probably are selling them privately for a quick sale, I am sure they perhaps wouldn't risk a car auction, but who knows and as far as paperwork is concerned the seller is long gone by then,' said DS Hodgson.

'This is bizarre, Jack, although I do recall something similar which happened to me a couple of years back but not on this grand scale. I was working in the drugs squad back then and we had a guy under surveillance for drug dealing. He had gone to the lengths of duplicating the exact vehicle he owned by buying another make and model which was identical in age, colour etc. and then re-plating it with his first vehicle's registration. He was now the proud owner of two identical vehicles. When we eventually arrested him, lo and behold, he brings out a fixed penalty ticket with a photograph that he had deliberately incurred which showed he was 100 miles away. This in fact proved to be his missus driving the duplicate vehicle who was shopping in York. We got him in the end, of course, but it just shows the lengths some of these criminals will go to,' remarked DS Webster.

'Fascinating, it's amazing what they will do to try and avoid detection,' said DS Hodgson, shaking his head.

'You mentioned CCTV recordings, have you managed to obtain these recordings from each car rental office?' enquired DS Webster.

'Yes, we have, Sarge, well to a degree anyway. Believe it or not some of the car rental companies actually overwrite their DVDs, drives, tapes etc. each night and some just have dummy CCTV cameras. The ones we have obtained have not really been focussed correctly so at this stage they are not a lot of use, we can't really get an image of the person who hires the car. In fact one hire company said they don't even bother recording on it, it's just a dummy camera for show, can you believe it!'

'You say person, have we not even identified whether it's a man or woman who hires the vehicles?'

'It varies, Sarge, and we haven't been able to get a specific description.'

'But presumably the person who hires the car pays up front before they are allowed to drive off?'

'Yes, that's correct, but we believe they are using stolen credit cards and some are using cash, which is making it even more difficult.'

'Ok, well thanks for that, I can't stop at present, Jack, but keep me posted on any developments, I really must dash. I have a meeting with DS Holdworth and the credit card fraud team in about 30 minutes,' said DS Webster, as he carefully edged his way past the cardboard boxes.

***

'I've had this wild idea, Tim,' said Charlie, as he downed his second pint.

'I'm not sure I like your wild ideas, Charlie, how wild is this one?' responded Tim.

'Look, we can only install these skimming devices in a limited number of locations and every time we do it we run the risk of getting caught, agreed?' said Charlie.

'Agreed,' said Tim, nodding his head.

'Well, my idea is this. Why don't we now use some of the money we've grabbed to date to buy more devices and rent them out, that way we don't take the risk and we can still earn a bob or two. It would be a sort of rent-to-own model for others who need to get their ATM thieving businesses started. They skim with our equipment and we get, say, 50% of the data they collect. We then sell the data we have just received. We could even setup a website on the dark web offering the equipment for hire, for example, the prospective ATM thief pays us, say, £1,000 as a deposit and we send them a skimmer and PIN pad overlay together with some basic instructions on installation and removal. They know they are getting a working skimmer and they send us the data back, what do you think?'

'I can see you've been thinking and applied your business studies degree,' said Tim, 'but we would have to encrypt the data somehow to make sure they had to send us the data back in the first place, otherwise they've got a cheap skimmer for next to nothing and buggered off with it. We would also need to make sure we don't create a duplicate of their data otherwise we will be selling on the same dumps of data. I think it's a brilliant idea, Charlie, it just needs carefully thinking through. We'll do it, it does need some planning, but leave it with me, as before that I have to get over to the café, I need to transfer some money, I'll see you later,' said Tim, finishing his drink.

***

Ted was wading through the boxes of CCTV recordings to try and discover the possible routes of some of the stolen vehicles. Some had just disappeared completely after passing through the ANPR cameras but suddenly, after what seemed endless hours of watching CCTV footage on specific vehicles, he spotted something of significant interest.

'Jack, come and take a look at this,' he shouted. 'I think we have our route, I have spent hours, even days, on this as you know, and I've kept notes on where each vehicle disappears. I'm convinced that we need to be looking in this area somewhere here, let me show you.'

Ted went over to the city map on the wall and drew a circle around a group of streets, saying confidently, 'This is roughly the area where we lose sight of the vehicles. Now not every missing vehicle uses the same route, of course, but they all seem to end in this area and we never see the vehicle again, it's a bit like the Bermuda Triangle. Correction, we never see the vehicle with that registration again, we haven't dared look at the volume in the area because we wouldn't know the registration plates they were using.'

'Right, good work, Ted, well, let's get a team together for tomorrow morning first thing, but in the meantime Pete, can you do some research and identify any possible properties, we are looking for, in particular, any vehicle business, car maintenance garages, lockups, MOT places, repair shops, that sort of thing in that area that Ted has marked out. I think the guys in the Command and Control centre can give you a head start, they will also have a list of key holders which will be useful,' said DC Hodgson, enthusiastically.

'Will do, Jack, I'm straight onto it,' said DC Bradley, logging into his computer.

CHAPTER 14

He caught the train to Birmingham New Street station, walked up Hill Street and found the internet café down a side street. It was virtually empty, apart from a couple of businessmen who were engrossed in some document or other in the corner. He had everything he needed; he logged into the bank account he'd been given, which was already setup with recipients' payment details, and transferred the sum of £3,000 to the bank account in Oldham.

He chuckled to himself when he thought how someone else's money was funding someone else's pain.

He logged off, did a spot of shopping in the Bull Ring and caught the next train back home.

CHAPTER 15

Dr Giles Stewart was attending a medical conference in Perth, Western Australia. He'd just arrived at Perth International Airport after a delayed nineteen hour flight from Manchester via Dubai. He'd been to Perth several times in the past: he loved the place and he had always promised his wife he would bring her there for a long holiday – but on this occasion he was travelling alone. It was late spring/early summer in Perth but already the temperatures had started climbing, and there was not a cloud in the azure sky as he walked across the tarmac in the warm sunshine from the plane into the terminal building.

He switched on his mobile phone whilst waiting for his bags to arrive on the conveyor belt in the arrival hall, and noticed that his wife had rung him several times. As it was still the middle of the night back in the UK he decided he would contact her later, and gave a wry smile as he decided it was probably something like the central heating boiler playing up again. It was strange how these things nearly always happened as soon as he went away!

After a short limousine ride from the airport he checked in at his favourite hotel, the Duxton on George Street. He asked for a room if possible overlooking the Swan River and across to South Perth. As he checked in, the clerk informed him that his wife had called the hotel several times and left a message for him to call her back as soon as possible. He checked his watch again and thought that, late or not, it must be urgent and so he picked up his key, took the lift to the seventh floor and rang his wife immediately after entering the room.

She told him that their credit card statement had arrived and there were transactions she thought were erroneous, as a result of which he had now exceeded his credit limit. 'That's impossible,' he replied. 'I hardly used it last month! My air fares, hotel deposits and everything needed for this trip were paid for by the company credit card over a week ago and I've paid the balance on mine from the previous month. You need to ring the bank as soon as possible and stop the card. Fortunately I have another card here that I can use. Please ring me back as soon as you have spoken with them.'

Dr Stewart went into shock. He'd had a long and tiring journey and although he'd had the luxury of travelling business class he needed some sleep. He was slumbering when his wife called him back to say that the bank had now blocked the card. The following day he was due to present his paper at the conference but he was certainly not in the best frame of mind.

***

DC Hodgson had had a sleepless night; he'd been up till all hours thinking about the next steps in the investigation. He arrived in the office early the next morning and, to his surprise, everyone was already there before him.

'Good God, have you lot soiled the bed or something! I thought I was in early,' he shouted across the office.

'Good afternoon, Jack! Very nice you could make it,' said Ted, grinning from behind his desk.

'Cheeky bugger! I bet you lot have been here all night,' replied DC Hodgson.

'Not quite, it just seems like that,' replied Ted. 'My eyes are a bit weary, I must admit. I could do with a couple of matchsticks to prop them open.'

'I've managed to bring in additional uniform resources from the local station, Jack, and I've arranged for them to meet us in Canal Street at 9.15am,' Pete added, 'so we'd better get a move on.'

'That's great, Pete. Did you also manage to get us a list of garages, storerooms and so on in the area? We have to start somewhere,' DC Hodgson replied.

'I have indeed, Jack,' said Pete, as he handed Jack copies of the list, which he was about to go through when his telephone rang.

'Hello, DC Hodgson here. How can I help?'

DC Hodgson looked somewhat shocked as he scribbled notes down whilst taking the call.

'And when was this you say, on Monday this week? Right, I'll get someone over to you to take a statement later today. Thank you for letting me know.'

'You won't believe this, guys – there's been another one. That was Midshire Car Hire,' said DC Hodgson, replacing the phone. 'They have a red Ford Mondeo which was hired and not returned four days ago. Can you get over there later on today, Pete, and get a statement from them? You know the sort of thing we want. In the meantime, everyone, we've got work to do. The uniform lads will be waiting for us down at Canal Street. Come on, Pete. Jean and Ted, can you please hold the fort? You can reach us on the mobiles if you need us. We have some premises to look at.'

DC Hodgson and DC Bradley arrived at the meeting point as arranged on Canal Street; they were assisted by four uniformed officers.

'Ok, here is a copy of the list,' said DC Hodgson. 'You take lower Canal Street and we'll take Bridgewater Way and split up if possible. We need to interview the key-holders of any of these properties on the list. If you see anything suspicious call me on the mobile straight away!'

They split up into three groups of two and after nearly two hours of what seemed to be a fruitless exercise DC Hodgson and DC Bradley found themselves interviewing the owner of three lock-up garages. They asked him to come with them and open each one in turn. On opening the second garage they found what they were looking for: a garage containing valeting cloths, cleaning materials, an old vacuum cleaner – but in particular a number of discarded car number plates.

'Bingo!' said DC Hodgson to the shocked garage owner. 'I think you have some explaining to do down at the station.'

'But I don't know anything! These aren't mine. I...' stammered the garage owner.

'Keep it for later, sir, when we are back at the station,' said DC Bradley as he accompanied him into their waiting car.

'Call the other teams, Pete, and tell them to stand down. I think we have found what we're looking for here,' said DC Hodgson. 'Lock this place up, and get SOCO over here as quickly as possible. The Midshire Car Rental company will have to wait for now – we've got an interview to do.'

In the distant shadows across the street was a figure watching their every move.

***

It was a quieter than normal morning in the Staffordshire offices of Andrew Brown's Estate Agents in the High Street in Biddulph. Business had been slow now for about two months but Rita Williams, the manager, was confident that the market would soon pick up again. It had to, she thought, or I'll be out of a job.

Just as she was making herself a cup of tea the phone rang and Rita took the call.

'Good morning. Andrew Brown's Estate Agents, Rita speaking. How can I help you?' she answered cheerily.

'Good morning. I'm looking to purchase a property in the Biddulph area and am interested in any semi-detached three-bedroom properties. Anything up to a maximum of a hundred thousand – and preferably properties which are ready to move into,' said the caller.

'Well, that shouldn't be a problem, sir. I'll see what we have on the books. I won't be a moment.' She put the phone down and walked across to the filing cabinet.

Two minutes later she came back and said, 'Yes, we have three properties ready to move into in that price bracket. Hello, hello!'

But to her surprise the line was dead and all she could hear was the dial tone.

***

Superintendent Jackson was busy at work that day; he had a number of meetings planned, one of which was with the Police and Crime Commissioner to discuss how they were going to tackle the new mobile app development. It was amazing how some of the senior officers assumed that the force IT department suddenly had all the necessary know-how and skills to develop mobile apps in-house. They clearly did not understand that this was a whole new area for the force to develop and could not be simply delivered overnight.

The Superintendent was reviewing his diary with his IT manager, John Edwards, when Samantha, his secretary, came in.

'I'm very sorry to disturb you, Superintendent, but Chief Inspector Newton and Inspector Downing from Professional Standards are here to see you. They are waiting outside.'

Superintendent Jackson looked somewhat shocked, and leafing quickly through his diary said, 'Really? I wasn't expecting anyone. You'd better send them in, Samantha.'

Minutes later Chief Inspector Newton and Inspector Downing came into the office.

'Good morning, Chief Inspector – and what can we do for PSD today?'

'Good morning again, Superintendent,' said the Chief Inspector, glancing over briefly at John Edwards.

'Can I introduce you to Inspector Downing? We have a delicate matter to discuss with you – so we would like to talk to you in private, if that's ok?'

The Superintendent nodded across to John Edwards to leave the office.

'Please close the door behind you, John. I shouldn't be too long here,' said the Superintendent confidently, as John Edwards got up to leave.

After what seemed to be an endless moment, whilst the Chief Inspector opened his briefcase and removed a large folder, the Superintendent himself eventually broke the silence. 'So, how can I help you, Chief Inspector? I don't have a great deal of spare time.'

'This is a difficult situation,' remarked the Chief Inspector, 'and there is no easy way to say this so I'll come straight to the point. As you know, we removed both your force laptop and your home laptop. The force laptop I am pleased to say is clean, no problems there. However, after examination of your home laptop by our Hi-Tech Crime unit, we have discovered a large number of pornographic images. We therefore have no option but to retain this evidence and suspend you from your duty pending further enquiries.'

'This is ridiculous, Chief Inspector! I have never downloaded pornographic images in my life. Someone here is trying to frame me! You have to believe me!'

And the Superintendent angrily banged the desk.

'That may be the case, sir, but you will be required to leave your desk immediately. You would be advised not to talk to anyone in the force and we will need to contact you in due course as our investigations progress. In the meantime I must tell you that, as from now, you are formally under suspension and we will need your warrant card,' said the Chief Inspector, somewhat coolly.

And with that the Superintendent got up from his desk, slammed his warrant card down, snatched his jacket from the coat rack, picked up his briefcase and left the two officers sitting there as he stamped out of the office in disgust.

CHAPTER 16

DC Hodgson and DC Bradley had returned to the local police station and were now interviewing Jim Iball, the owner of the lock-up garage where seven pairs of number plates had been found. All were the original plates from stolen hire cars.

'Now then, Mr. Iball, so how can you explain the presence of these number plates that we found in your garage yesterday morning?' asked DC Hodgson, as he lined them up like soldiers across the floor.

'Look, I keep telling you; although the garage belongs to me, I have rented it out. I rent them all out! It's my livelihood – and I have no idea how those number plates got there. I have never seen them before. I mean, I can't be held responsible for whatever my tenants keep in the garages, can I? I keep telling you, why don't you believe me? It was rented to someone else.'

'Well, we simply don't believe you because you can't prove to us that it is rented. There's no paperwork, no evidence, no trace whatsoever, in fact no someone else to show that you have rented it out,' said DC Bradley, raising his voice.

'Look, it was a cash transaction. I keep telling you, this bloke, I don't even know what his name is, just turned up one day and paid me in notes up front about four months ago for a six month rent. It would have been about four hundred and eighty pounds. I didn't ask him his name, or what he wanted it for. It's none of my business. I haven't even seen him since.'

'So, we would see that amount being paid into your bank account then, would we?' said DC Bradley, pointing his finger. 'Perhaps we should make arrangements to recover your bank statements?'

'Erm, well, no, erm… it went into my petty cash box.'

'Are you seriously expecting us to believe that you deposited four hundred and eighty in petty cash?'

'Well, it's the truth, I'm telling you. Why won't you believe me?'

'Now look, Mr. Iball, if it helps at all, I actually do believe you – but you must give us more information.'

DC Hodgson was looking to play the good cop.

'Look, I've told you all that I know. Why don't you believe me?'

Jim Iball put his head in his hands. 'I can't possibly know what was in there or be responsible for what people keep in their garages.'

'Is there anything you can remember about this person who rented the garage, any little thing which you might recall, no matter how insignificant you think it might be?' asked DC Hodgson.

'Well, I did have a job understanding him a bit,' said Jim Iball.

'How do you mean, you had a job understanding him? Was he mumbling or something?'

DC Hodgson suddenly sat up.

'Well, he had a strange accent,' came the reply.

***

Tim and Charlie had established what they found was a very lucrative business. They were now renting skimmers and pin pads across the country to other would-be thieves on a regular basis.

They had held off from planting any further skimming devices for themselves for the time being and were now firmly set up as Thunderbird2 and 3 as suppliers in the dark web cyber forum.

Planting an ATM skimmer to intercept credit and debit card data was clearly a risky venture because the thieves, of course, had to return to the scene of their crime to recover them. The undercover market on the cyber forum for skimming devices was now buoyant and in some cases would-be thieves parted with significant amounts of money only to find they had bought a bogus device, which was nothing more than a piece of hardware and did nothing except look like the real thing.

Tim, as Thunderbird2, however, had now gathered somewhat of a following and he had struck a deal with his supplier in the Far East. He had since managed to embed his own encryption code into the skimming device. This meant that thieves renting the skimmer from him had no option but to send the data back to him for decryption of the card details they had stolen. He had thieves queuing up for them and soon the two of them were also trading in credit card data without taking the risk of being found out planting or recovering the devices.

The said devices were being improved all the time and Tim was getting greedier as the days rolled by. He was now working on a way of using ATM skimmers that relayed the data back to him automatically via a text message.

But banks were not standing still and those which had previously been hit with skimming devices were now building in plastic covers to prevent hidden cameras photographing pin number entry. The criminals' speedy response was to replicate them with a hidden camera in the cover. In other words, as fast as the banks were developing security devices to overcome thieves, the criminals were very quick to find new innovative ways around them.

Tim thought he was foolproof.
But how wrong could he be?

***

Peter Owen had just arrived at London Euston railway station on the Virgin Pendolino train from Manchester. He had arranged a series of meetings in the capital over the next three days, which he had booked with potential clients who were very interested in his clothing range. The Owen family had a respectable clothing and textiles business in Manchester which had been in the family for well over a hundred years, and they were doing well, despite the current recession. The company, which had been started by Peter's grandfather, had seen highs and lows over the decades but had done well in maintaining its position as suppliers of high quality men's clothing. Things had also changed somewhat since his grandfather's days and clothing which had previously been made in their own factories in the Oldham area was now manufactured in the Far East. They had been a large, respected employer in the area but the move of manufacturing base had resulted in the workforce diminishing in the UK from over a hundred to just under ten staff. Peter was therefore now a regular traveller to Hong Kong, where the bulk of their men's suits were made and purchased. On this occasion he was in sales mode, however, and he took a taxi to the Thistle Hotel at Marble Arch. He was in the process of checking in when the check-in assistant asked him for a credit card for the booking.

'Certainly,' said Peter taking his card from his wallet. 'It's a MasterCard,' and handed it over to the assistant.

The assistant placed the card in the card reader which resulted immediately in the unexpected message of 'Not valid Refused/Declined – please contact MasterCard' being displayed on the reader.

'I am sorry, sir,' said the assistant politely, 'but this card is not valid. Do you have another one you could use?'

'Not valid! Are you quite sure?' replied Peter. 'That's ridiculous! I used it a couple of days ago to book my train fare down here. Are you sure? Can you please try it again?'

'Well, I'm sorry sir, but it appears to have been blocked. We will need another card.'

Peter fortunately had another card in his wallet and this worked satisfactorily. He collected his bedroom key and immediately called MasterCard on his mobile as a matter of urgency.

CHAPTER 17

Four Weeks Later

Alan Jackson was now getting used to being at home full-time. His large front and back gardens had never looked so tidy and he was less stressed than normal. He had joined a local gym and found a new group of friends through regular lunch time visits to his local public house. He hadn't heard anything from PSD apart from when they turned up one day unexpectedly to ask him a few further questions and to say they were continuing to hold on to his laptop as retained evidence. He assumed they were continuing to investigate who could have planted the pornographic images on his laptop and he thought it would be just a matter of time before he'd be invited back to his old job as Head of Information Technology at Police HQ.

He had decided to give the front lawn a final cut for the winter and was trimming the edges when an unmarked police car turned up. It was Chief Inspector Newton and another officer whom he didn't recognise and hadn't seen before.

'Good morning, sir,' said Chief Inspector Newton, getting out of the car. 'I'm sorry to disturb you, and we can see you are very busy, but can we have a quiet word inside?'

'Yes, of course, Chief Inspector. I would, however, have appreciated a call to say you were coming. I hope you're bringing me good news and that I can return to work?'

Superintendent Jackson switched off his lawn edger.

The police officers didn't immediately respond to Alan Jackson's question and followed him inside and sat down in the lounge.

'In answer to your question sir, the answer is no. I'm afraid we can't let you return to work just yet. I'm also sorry, sir – we should have called you to arrange to meet, but assumed you would be home. May I introduce you to Inspector Wilbraham? She is the investigating officer working on the case at PSD,' said the Chief Inspector, opening his folder.

'I'll come straight to the point, Superintendent. As you know, we have been investigating your case and there have been some further developments which we need to discuss with you. If I can return to when we were first informed of the messages on Crime Stoppers that it was alleged you were selling pornographic images online and…'

'Yes, yes, I've told you about that. It is preposterous! It is completely untrue, a complete pack of lies.'

Superintendent Jackson was now rather angry.

'Yes, I understand how you feel, Superintendent Jackson, but you must realise…' the Chief Inspector began.

'I realise nothing, Chief Inspector. Why it has taken you all this time to investigate this pack of lies is beyond me,' said Superintendent Jackson interrupting him.

'Yes, but you must realise we have to investigate all the allegations,' replied the Chief Inspector. 'If I may continue – well, as I was saying, there have been some developments.'

'You've found who was responsible?' interjected the Superintendent.

'No, I'm afraid not, but I will leave Inspector Wilbraham to outline these developments,' said the Chief Inspector, who was somewhat annoyed by the constant interruptions and had decided to hand over the conversation.

'Well, Superintendent Jackson, the developments relate to certain bank transactions, and, in particular, amounts that have been transferred to one of your bank accounts over the past three months. These amounts are quite considerable and in fact almost ten thousand pounds was placed in one of your savings accounts,' said Inspector Wilbraham.

'What! I don't have that sort of amount in any of my savings accounts. Most of my money is invested in stocks and shares, so you must be mistaken,' said Superintendent Jackson.

'No, there's no mistake, Superintendent. We have double checked the dates and the amounts, and you do have this amount in your savings account.'

'That's impossible! I'm being set up here. I have no idea who is behind these transactions. I didn't even know about them. I mean, I only get these statements annually.'

'Well, that's as maybe, but I'm sure you must understand that this puts a whole different perspective on things – and the matter has also been referred to the National Police Complaints Board as a matter of course. It is highly likely that the investigation will now be carried out by a different police force. In the meantime, if you can add anything to the investigation, then please contact me,' said Chief Inspector Newton, getting up to go.

'This has become a nightmare. Someone is definitely out to put me in the frame for something I haven't done – and I think it's about time that I find out who,' said Alan Jackson, as he got up to see the officers out.

'Now, don't take anything on yourself, Superintendent. You'll be advised to leave well alone. Leave this investigation to us. We'll be in touch. We'll see ourselves out. Goodbye for now,' said the Chief Inspector as they left the hallway.

'Leave it to you! That's a laugh! You've taken weeks to get this far!'

Alan Jackson slammed the door behind them.

And he had already started thinking about who could be responsible for putting him through all this.

***

Richard Evans drove into the Divisional HQ car park and parked up his Honda CRV in what he thought was an unallocated car parking space. Sod it, he thought, I've had a long commute into work and I'm fed up driving around here trying to find a space. The space was marked Fraud Team and he got out, locked the car and made his way across the car park in the pouring rain. Richard was the Crime Analyst working on secondment to the Card Fraud Investigation team at Midshire Police on Operation Trident. He was new to both the team and the Midshire Police but he had shown considerable promise and was a dedicated individual. He was highly thought of by his boss, the Principal Analyst Barbara Smith, who had recruited him from the private sector.

He was normally based in the southern area of the force but in his new seconded role to the Card Fraud Investigation team he now had to travel over forty miles daily to his office, something he was not happy with as he couldn't claim mileage expenses [for some strange reason only known to the Finance department].

The force had seen a notable increase in reported card fraud over the past few weeks yet the Crime Statistics didn't appear to show this. Richard had been drafted in to help the team with their increasing workload.

He thought it was strange that the Home Office counting rules, from a statistics point of view, didn't seem to tally with the number of victims. Presumably because Card Fraud victims were being reimbursed by their banks for amounts stolen by thieves. Nevertheless, it was recognised in the force that the workload in their team had risen significantly over the past few months and they were now determined to identify the offenders. The new investigation system had been designed to assist them with this and every piece of data, including the possible locations where cards had been stolen, was now being recorded. The force had a policy that every piece of data was important and this was reflected in the design of the new triggering module in their new investigation system.

The triggering module was new to the force and very innovative as all data was subject to being monitored overnight across the crime-related systems. This meant that departments would automatically be alerted if something or someone had been mentioned in one system that had also occurred in another.

Richard walked into the Operation Trident office, poured himself a coffee from the pot in the kitchen and was now deep in conversation with one of his colleagues on the pros and cons of pattern detection of credit card scams that had emerged in the force area recently.

Suddenly the door burst open and a sodden DS Holdsworth appeared.

'Ok, you lot, which bugger is parked in my parking space? Come on, own up! It must be one of you! I've had to park outside down the road in the multi-storey car park which is going to cost me twelve quid today. And I've got bloody soaked walking up here! Come on, own up! I've asked all the others next door. Come on – who owns a silver Honda CRV?'

There was silence from everyone shrugging their shoulders except for Richard, who looked slightly baffled.

'Well, come on then – is anyone going to cough to it?'

'Erm… that might be me. Sorry, sir, I hadn't realised it was allocated to anyone in particular. I thought it was available to anyone,' said Richard, sheepishly.

The rest of the office staff kept their heads down; DS Holdsworth had quite a temper and could blow up at the least little thing.

'Available to anyone! It's taken me twenty years to get a bloody spot in that car park! Well, I'll let it go this time as you are new to the team, Richard. But the space is allocated to me personally – and don't any of you forget it,' said DS Holdsworth, shaking off his jacket and picking up the mail from his desk.

'This has not got me off to a good start this morning to be honest. I'm bloody drenched! But if you make me a coffee, milk with two sugars, we'll say no more about it,' said DS Holdsworth, lightening up and winking at DC Winterbottom. He opened one of his letters and did a speed read of its contents while Richard brought him a coffee.

'You are working on trends and patterns, aren't you Richard? Here, have a look at this. I've just received it from our Force Intelligence Department with reference to a new trend we are encountering.'

Richard picked up the letter and studied it in much more detail than DS Holdsworth had.

'That's interesting,' he said. 'A new type of credit card scam emerging over recent weeks whereby holders of the cards are in the early months of paying the balance off monthly in full, building up a high credit card limit, thus clocking up a huge debt – and then disappearing without trace. I must admit I haven't come across that one before. That's a new one on me. Anyway, we'll log the occurrences into the investigative database and keep an eye on it. In the meantime, I'll get back to trying to identify the patterns on these ATM scams which seem to be on the rise.'

'Maybe you should move your car before then,' said DS Holdsworth, as he sipped his coffee.

CHAPTER 18

The Operation Carousel team were having their monthly review of the investigation and were deep in discussion and summarising where they now were with everything. The investigation had been running for six weeks and at least there was one thing which was positive – the non-return of hire cars had stopped for some reason and in fact they hadn't had an occurrence for over a month. This may have been down to the fact that the car hire companies were tightening up on rentals but it was also possible that the offenders had now gone underground.

'This is not good, team. I need to present this when I meet with the DCI tomorrow afternoon for his progress meeting, and so far he'll be thinking that we've been in the pub every lunchtime,' said DC Hodgson.

'He won't be far wrong then, Jack,' Ted replied, sarcastically.

'Thanks, Ted, for your kind support, you bugger! Anyway, back to the job in hand. So, let me summarise the situation as I see it. We have identified only one vehicle so far that has been definitely cloned. The others – well, we have no idea where they are. They could still be in lock-up garages, they could be driven around the country somewhere under different number plates or, for all we know, possibly even transported overseas. What we need to do now is follow up on finding the driver, or indeed the owner, of the Mike Johnson cloned vehicle –

which could be anywhere. He or she must have some clues. I want to know where they have bought it from, who sold it to them, how much they paid for it, and do they have any paperwork to back up the sale. I have put out an alert to all forces that, if they spot the registration, to get back in touch with us. Of course we are going to get several false identifications of Mike Johnson's own car but that's inevitable and can't be helped.'

'Now, as regards that lock-up garage, have we got anywhere, Pete, with Jim Iball, the owner?'

'Nowhere, Jack. The only piece of information that he could provide us with was that whoever rented the garage had a strange accent. It's not a lot of use I'm afraid. We don't even have a description. He says it was dark! I'm still suspicious of him, Jack. He's not giving us anything to go on and I think he's holding back on something.'

Pete had clearly taken a dislike to Jim Iball!

'What about SOCO? Did they turn anything up?

'Well, after we'd left they were all over the scene, as you know. We did get some fingerprints off the number plates that were found and these are being checked as we speak. There was nothing else worth noting,' replied DC Bradley.

'Well, that just about sums up where we are then,' DC Hodgson replied gloomily.

'Not quite,' interjected Jean. 'Jack, do you remember that last incident we had? You know, the one when you took the phone call, from Midshire Car Rental? Well, our checks show that the person who hired the vehicle there used a credit card for payment.'

'That's great – and do we have the details of the card owner, Jean?'

'We do indeed, Jack. I obtained the details this morning. It was hired by a Dr Giles Stewart of Wrexham, North Wales,' replied Jean.

'Right, Pete, find out the full address of our Mr. Stewart. Ted, inform North Wales Police we are coming on their patch to interview him – and we'll get over there straight away.'

'It's *Doctor* Stewart, Jack,' prompted Ted, correcting him.

'Doctor or Mister, let's find out a bit more about him as soon as possible. It's your turn to drive, Pete. Come on, we've no time to waste. We might even get to sample the waters in the local hostelry,' replied DC Hodgson, with a wry grin.

***

'Would you mind getting out of the car please, sir?' said the young police officer.

'Not again,' said Mike Johnson. 'I can't believe it! This is the third time this week.'

'I'm sorry, sir, but your vehicle has been flagged up by PNC as an alert,' said the young traffic officer. 'Are you the owner of this car, sir?'

'Yes, I mean no.'

'Well, which is it sir, are you or aren't you?'

'It's no, actually. It's owned by the company I work for, Northern Computer Services. It's a company car assigned to me,' replied Mike, somewhat irritably.

'Do you have the driving documents to support this, sir? Driving licence, insurance and registration documents?'

'Yes, I have my driving licence with me but I will need to get copies of the company's insurance documents as they are kept in the office.'

Mike Johnson handed over his driving licence from his wallet.

'Thank you, sir. You will need to present your other documents to any police station within the next seven days,' said the police officer, handing back the driving licence.

'Yes, yes, yes, I know the procedure, officer. I already plan to do that from my previous stop and search, officer,' said Mike, trying to maintain his composure.

'Oh, one more thing, would you mind opening the boot for me, sir?'

'Not at all. I think you'll find there is absolutely nothing of interest there except my golf clubs. No dead bodies or illegal immigrants!'

'Yes, very funny sir. Well, all seems to be ok. Nice car, this. I wouldn't mind one of these myself,' said the officer, closing the boot.

Mike Johnson thought, you can have this one if I keep getting stopped in it.

'Very well, sir, everything seems to be in order. You are free to continue your journey now, but don't forget to call in at the police station with your documents.'

'How can I forget when you are stopping me all the time?' thought Mike Johnson, as he drove off, now in a bad mood and late for his appointment.

CHAPTER 19

Dr Giles Stewart had not enjoyed the conference in Perth. His presentation had not gone down as well as expected with delegates and he realised his mind had not been fully focussed on the event. He had spent months preparing his paper on the 'Functional vitamin B_{12} deficiency and Alzheimer disease' and prior to his trip he had everything in place for his presentation. He was quietly confident, having given the same talk at previous conferences over the past two years. It was probably a combination of jet lag from the flight from Manchester and his stolen credit card details which was preying on his mind, which resulted in the fact that he didn't give the talk to the best of his ability. His credit card had now been blocked by MasterCard, the thieves having clocked up a total of £10,500 over a very short period, and he had resorted to using another of his cards to pay for the hotel and expenses in Australia.

Giles was now en route home via Dubai. At least he could sit back, relax and enjoy the service on the Emirates A380 on the upper deck in business class and all he wanted to do now was to get home to see his wife, Joan.

On arrival at Manchester Airport he collected his bags from the carousel [fortunately they were the first ones to arrive] and headed to the meeting point, where the airline chauffeur was waiting to drive him home to Wrexham.

He managed to keep the conversation between himself and the driver to an absolute minimum and on the M56 he pretended to doze off in the back of the car, ignoring every opportunity for conversation that the driver attempted to bring up.

Soon they had left the A55 and crossed into Wales and shortly afterwards the Mercedes limo turned into his road. He couldn't help but notice that there was a strange car parked in the driveway. He thought it must be one of Joan's friends from work. He retrieved his bags from the boot, tipped the driver and let himself in through the front door.

'Oh, is that you love?' said Mrs Stewart from the kitchen. 'We have some visitors in the lounge who are waiting to see you. I'll be through in a minute. I'm just making some tea.'

'Hi love! Yes, it's me, back from down under and I need a cup of tea – I'm quite parched.' Giles dropped his bags at the foot of the stairs and walked into the lounge.

There sitting in the lounge were two men who immediately stood up and introduced themselves.

'Ah, good evening. It's Doctor Stewart, I believe? My name is DC Hodgson and this is my colleague, DC Bradley from Midshire Police. We are sorry to trouble you, as we understand you've had a long journey home and you must be very tired, but we have a number of questions we need to ask you, if that's ok?'

'Really? Yes, I am tired, officer, but please go ahead. How can I help you?'

Giles Stewart removed his jacket and carefully placed it over a dining room chair.

'Well, we understand you hired a car from Midshire Car Rental a few weeks ago, a red Ford Mondeo?' said DC Hodgson.

'Did I? You must be mistaken, officer? I don't think so. On what date was this supposed to have happened?' said Giles, with a puzzled expression.

'It was the 31$^{st of}$ October,' piped up DC Bradley.

'No, not me,' replied Giles, shaking his head.

'There's no mistake, Dr Stewart, these are the details we have from Midshire Car Rental,' said DC Bradley.

'I assure you, officer, I have not hired a rental car from Midshire Car Rental, whoever they are supposed to be. I've never even heard of them. The last car I hired was in Perth last week.'

'Well, it was hired with your credit card and that is the information we have here,' said DC Bradley.

'Ah, I think I can see what may have happened here. My credit card details were stolen just prior to me going away. My wife has reported it to MasterCard, who have now blocked it.'

'When do you think your details were stolen, sir? And did you not think of reporting it to the police?'

'Well, clearly not, I'm afraid. I have been in Australia for a couple of weeks and I discovered on my arrival there that my card details had been stolen. My wife informed MasterCard who blocked it immediately. She discovered it only when our card statement arrived while I was away and I have obviously not had time to inform you.'

'I see. Did you actually lose your card, sir?'

'No. It appears I have been a victim of ID theft. Whoever it is clearly has my credit card details. I still have the actual card in my wallet,' replied Giles.

'It does, indeed. Well, thank you, sir, and we are sorry to have troubled you. May I suggest you now destroy that card, Dr. Stewart. Have you any idea where your card details could have been stolen? Online shopping, restaurants, petrol stations for example?'

'No, I can't think where they could have picked the details up, officer. I never shop online and I always make sure I can see my card when it's being processed, at a shop for example. I never withdraw cash at a cashpoint as they charge commission. I mainly use it for petrol, and it's been a nightmare couple of weeks, I can tell you.'

'I am sure it has, sir. Once again, thanks very much for your time – and we'll leave you in peace to catch up on some sleep,' said DC Hodgson, as they both got up to leave.

'Thank you, officers, and sorry we didn't inform you of the incident,' said Dr Stewart, closing the front door behind them.

***

Frank and Mary Renwick were travelling into Newton Stewart in the beautiful region of Dumfries and Galloway on the Monday morning to do their weekly shop. Frank was a retired headmaster and a stickler for discipline; he'd been retired now for ten years and was in good health, apart from being severely troubled with arthritis which made him grumpier than normal. His arthritis had now got to the stage where he was in constant pain and had some difficulty at times in walking.

They always left their shopping until a Monday as it was quieter and they could get around the aisles of the supermarket more easily. Most weeks they would leave the car in the garage and take the bus into town. The bus dropped them off right outside the supermarket, which was very convenient.

On this particular morning the weather hadn't been too kind so they decided to drive into town. They had just driven into the supermarket car park when Frank noticed that he was being followed by a police car. He parked in the disabled bay close to the store entrance and they got out and he locked the car. The police car drove into the next disabled bay, and Frank was about to tell the officer that the parking bays were for disabled customers only when the officer approached him.

'Excuse me sir, are you the owner of this vehicle?' enquired the young police officer politely.

'Yes, I am officer. Is there a problem?' replied Frank, who was taken aback.

'Can I see your driving licence, sir?

'Certainly, officer. I should have it here somewhere.'

Frank, after some fumbling in his wallet, managed to find his driving licence and handed it to the officer.

'That all seems to be in order, sir. Do you have your insurance and registration documents with you?'

'Not with me, officer. The insurance policy is at home and I'm currently awaiting the registration documents.'

'I see. So, how long have you owned this vehicle?' said the officer.

'We've owned the vehicle since, well, it must be just about a month ago, officer. We bought it from someone in Dumfries. We are very pleased with it. Is there a problem, officer? I drive very slowly these days so I shouldn't think I've been speeding.'

The police officer didn't answer and continued to make notes.

'Is there a problem, officer? Have we done something wrong?'

Mary repeated the question nervously.

'Well, you see, madam, your vehicle is on an alert on PNC, hence the reason I stopped you. If you could just wait here for a moment, I'll need to check something with my sergeant back at the station.'

The police officer walked off about ten yards from them and radioed into the station to inform his sergeant that he had stopped an alerted vehicle. Five minutes later he returned to the Renwicks who were waiting patiently, standing with their vehicle.

'Sorry to keep you, Mr. and Mrs. Renwick, but we will need you to present your vehicle documents at your nearest police station within seven days. We will also need to contact you further to discuss when and where you purchased the vehicle. In the meantime please continue with your shopping and someone will be in touch,' said the officer, climbing back in his car.

'Well, I wonder what all that was about?' said Mary, looking puzzled.

'It beats me, Mary. I reckon it must be some sort of mistake on their computer. Come on, let's go and do the shopping. My legs are starting to play up just standing here,' replied Frank.

CHAPTER 20

Tim Ridgway had just moved into his new, fully furnished, penthouse apartment in the centre of Manchester. Money was now rolling in from a number of the illegal schemes he was working on. The rent-a-skimmer model he and Charlie came up with had been put into operation and the skimming device had been modified to capture card details which were then encrypted. The data was then sent via text to one of Tim's mobiles, which was constantly plugged into a USB port on one of his laptops, and these were then downloaded into his laptop. The only honest thing he was now doing was emailing 50% of the data back to the hirers of the skimming device.

The remaining card details were then sold as 'lists' or 'dumps' to other thieves in return for bitcoins. He continued to share the proceeds of this with Charlie, who was concentrating on further developing their illegal business. They had trialled the pay-at-the-pump skimming device for a short while and, although it worked satisfactorily, it presented problems with installation so they had abandoned that idea.

Charlie was working one night as normal and he'd decided to dress as a workman pretending to service the petrol pump. He'd gone out on the forecourt when the garage was quiet and had nearly wrecked the petrol pump by taking it apart but was unable to re-assemble it – so they gave it up as a bad idea.

Since that incident Charlie had packed in his job at the petrol station and had moved into an up-market apartment in Manchester, around the corner from Tim's penthouse. They were both driving near new Mercedes C Class saloons and partying at Tim's place on a regular basis.

***

DC Hodgson was in work early that morning; he couldn't sleep as the investigation didn't seem to be getting anywhere and he knew he would be under pressure soon to find some results. In summary, Operation Carousel was running cold and both DS Webster and DCI Bentley were getting rather impatient for answers. In fact, with no further occurrences of hire car theft, the DCI was thinking of closing the case as unsolved.

'Let's go over that again, Pete,' said DC Hodgson. 'The only vehicle that has been stopped in three weeks by police across the UK with the number plates we are monitoring is Mike Johnson's actual car – and I'm sure he must be getting absolutely fed up with being stopped.'

'Well, it appears that way. It's dried up completely now, Jack, as Northern Computer Services have agreed to temporarily take the vehicle off the road. It was getting beyond a joke and Mr Johnson is now driving a hire car.'

'At least he must be happy that he's not being stopped,' said Ted.

'I wouldn't say he's happy, Ted. The firm have given him an old Ford Fiesta instead of his new Mondeo as a temporary replacement car!'

'So, we are back to square one. We thought we had a lead with Dr Stewart's credit card but that took us nowhere – other than the fact that these vehicles are probably being hired using stolen credit cards. Jim Iball has been no help whatsoever in identifying the person who hired his garage. The fingerprint check from the discarded number plates drew a blank. I can't think where we go from here,' said DC Hodgson.

Just then his telephone rang.

'Get that, will you Pete? I'm just trying to complete this report for the DCI,' said DC Hodgson.

'Good morning. Midshire Police, DC Bradley speaking. How I can I help you?'

'Ah, good morning, this is PC Urqhart from Dumfries Police. We understand you have put an alert out on a Ford Mondeo. Is that correct?' said the voice on the other end.

'Yes, that's correct. Have you spotted the vehicle?'

'We have indeed. It belongs to a Mr Frank Renwick of Wishaw Villas in Newton Stewart. He bought the vehicle about a month ago apparently. We have checked his paperwork and it's all in order apart from the V5C vehicle registration document which he is currently waiting for. Mr Renwick is a retired headmaster and we have informed him that the police will need to come and question him.'

'That's fantastic news! Thanks very much. Goodbye for now,' said DC Bradley, putting the phone down.

'You said we don't know where we go from here, Jack. Well, I do! Come on – we're off to bonnie Scotland!'

Alan Jackson was pleased with the new laptop that he had just bought. He had tired of waiting for the return of his old one as the police were still retaining it. At least now he could try to do his own research into who it was that was actually trying to frame him. Over the past few weeks he'd decided to keep away from accessing email and he found he actually didn't miss being online. It was back to life as he knew it before the internet. Anybody who wanted him could reach him by the phone. It also gave him the chance to do other jobs around the house and, in particular, spend more time gardening.

He logged in that morning for the first time in weeks and accessed his email account, which was now showing 561 unread emails, most of which were junk. He still went through each email one by one to make sure, deleting them as he went, and he was horrified to discover that he was now receiving emails from people he had never even heard of, asking to buy pornographic material from him.

He decided to move those particular emails into a separate folder and deleted everything else. He decided it was time for action and to start investigating who was behind this campaign to completely discredit him.

He could not call on his colleagues in Midshire Police while he was suspended, so, who could he call? His hand hovered over the telephone and, after a short while, he decided to phone an old friend of his, Jeff Reynolds, who had worked for him in the past in the Computer Department. Jeff had retired a few years previously and he was a bit of a whizz-kid when it came to computers. The term 'whizz pensioner' didn't seem quite right somehow.

'Hi Jeff, it's Alan Jackson here. Long time no speak! I wonder if we could meet up for a beer in the next day or two? I need some help urgently. I'll explain why when we meet up but is there any chance we can get together at my place tomorrow at two o'clock and we can then go on to the White Lion for lunch? That's great. I'll see you then.'

Alan replaced the receiver and logged back onto his laptop as he sat back in his chair and thought about what he needed to prepare for his meeting with Jeff.

***

DC Hodgson and DC Bradley had travelled up to Scotland by car. It had taken them nearly five hours, with delays on the M6 near Bamber Bridge. Ted had found a hotel for them online and booked them both into what he described as a charming hotel on the outskirts of Newton Stewart.

'It looks a bit smaller than the photograph on the website, Jack,' said DC Bradley, as they drove into the hotel car park.

'Look, it's only for one night, Pete. We should be able to get what we need from Mr and Mrs Renwick and then we can try to contact the person who sold them the car.'

'Well, if the car park is anything to go by, then the rooms can't be up to much! The term car park is pushing it a bit – it's more like a three car layby! My driveway at home is bigger than this.'

They stood for a few minutes looking at the grey stone building and rotting window frames. The hotel had clearly seen better days and was in much need of care and attention to the paintwork. They made their way across the car park, pushed open the stiff oak door and

111

entered the hallway. There was not a soul about, but eventually, after ringing a bell on the reception desk several times, an old gentleman arrived to sign them in.

'Good afternoon, how may I help you?' said the old gentleman, who looked as though he had just woken from an afternoon doze in the armchair.

'Mr Hodgson and Mr Bradley. We are booked in for one night,' said DC Hodgson, who didn't want to announce that they were police officers.

'Ah, yes,' said the old gentleman. 'You must be the police officers from Midshire Police. Here are the keys. Your rooms are ready. I've put DC Hodgson in room one and you, DC Bradley, are in room three. You will find the bathroom at the end of the corridor. You might have difficulty with the shower in the morning. I have called the plumber but it's anybody's guess when he'll arrive!'

Thanks, Ted, thought DC Hodgson as he took his room key.

After checking in and dropping their bags off in their rooms they decided to grab a late lunch and went in for a quick bite in the café next door.

'How is your room, Pete?' enquired Jack.

'Put it this way Jack, it's a good job I didn't bring a cat with me! There isn't room for one!' chuckled Pete.

They finished their meal and headed straight for Wishaw Villas to interview Frank and Mary Renwick. The Renwicks lived the other end of town in a well-to-do area. On arrival at the house, the officers saw in the driveway the duplicate Ford Mondeo they had been looking for. It was in pristine condition as Frank had been cleaning it at least twice a week; it was his pride and joy.

DC Hodgson rang the doorbell and after a couple of minutes Mary Renwick opened the door.

'Good afternoon, Mrs Renwick, I'm DC Hodgson from Midshire Police and this is my colleague, DC Bradley. We wish to speak to you about the car that you and your husband have recently bought,' said DC Hodgson, showing his ID.

'Good afternoon, officer. Yes, we were told that we may get a call from you. Please come in,' said Mary, who then shouted upstairs to her husband, 'Frank, there are two police officers here to see us. I think it must be about the car.'

The officers were led into a very nice conservatory overlooking the immaculately kept rear garden.

'Do sit down. Would you both like a cup of tea?' asked Mary.

'No thank you, Mrs Renwick. We are fine – we have just had one,' replied DC Hodgson.

Just as they sat down Frank Renwick came in. 'Good afternoon, officers. I'm Frank Renwick. I gather you wish to see me about the car.'

'Yes. Good afternoon, Mr Renwick. We understand you recently bought a red Ford Mondeo, registration JX12YUV,' said DC Bradley, looking at his notes.

'That's right – you've just passed it in the driveway,' replied Frank.

DC Bradley immediately thought back for a moment to the comment made by Mike Johnson.

'And where exactly did you buy the vehicle, Mr Renwick?' DC Hodgson asked.

'I saw it advertised in the local paper and I rang the mobile number. A very nice young man answered. I think he said his name was James Smith. He brought the car round to us. It was the easiest way I've ever bought a car. We'd already sold our old one privately and it was a very good deal,' replied Frank Renwick.

DC Hodgson's heart sank as he realised it would be very unlikely that the trail would continue from here.

'Can you give us a description of him?' said DC Bradley.

'Well, he was taller than me. I'd put him at about five feet ten inches, very well spoken,' replied Frank.

'Can you remember what he was wearing?'

'Yes, I think he was wearing a blue anorak – you know, one of the expensive types. It had some sort of red badge on one of the sleeves. I think he had jeans and quite smart brown shoes,' said Mary Renwick.

DC Bradley continued to make notes.

'Could we now have a quick look at the vehicle, Mr Renwick?' said DC Bradley.

'Yes, of course. I've got the car keys with me.'

They went back out into the driveway and Mr Renwick opened the car for them.

'Could you open the bonnet please, Mr Renwick? We just need to take a quick look.'

Frank Renwick did as he was asked and immediately DC Hodgson spotted the amateur-looking VIN Chassis number plate which had been glued on but was now starting to peel off, revealing the original chassis number plate. DC Bradley made a note of both numbers and they closed the bonnet.

'Right, Mr Renwick, I think we've seen enough out here. If we can just go inside for a moment, we have a few more questions to ask you and your wife.'

They went back into the conservatory and sat down; DC Hodgson paused for a while before speaking.

'Well, I'm afraid it's as we thought, Mr and Mrs Renwick. The car you have bought is in fact a stolen vehicle and the registration is not the correct one. You have bought what is called a cloned vehicle. It has the number plates from another car.'

Frank and Mary Renwick were now going into a state of shock.

'But we had no idea we were buying a cloned vehicle! We handed over £9,500 in cash for it and it seemed such a bargain. He told us that he'd bought the car recently from new and was emigrating to Australia - hence the reason for selling it cheaply. I thought it was taking longer than usual for the registration document to arrive. I assume we can keep it with its original registration?' Mary Renwick replied.

'No, I'm afraid not, Mrs Renwick. The vehicle will have to be collected and returned back to its rightful owners, which we believe is a car hire company back in Manchester,' said DC Hodgson.

'I'm afraid handling stolen goods is a crime, Mr Renwick, but you're unlikely to be arrested as you clearly didn't know the car had been stolen,' said DC Bradley.

'Can I still drive it until it's collected?' asked Frank Renwick, who was clearly upset by the whole thing.

'Well, no, I'm afraid not. If you do carry on driving it, you could be arrested for handling stolen goods,' replied DC Hodgson.

'But will we get our money back?' asked Mary Renwick.

'It's unlikely, I'm afraid. If you wish to get your money back, you would need to take the person who sold you the car to court – and that is going to be easier said than done. It is very unlikely that you will be able to trace the young man who sold it to you.'

Mary Renwick went white and suddenly felt sick.

'£9,500 pounds down the drain, just like that,' said Frank Renwick, shaking his head and putting his arm around Mary.

'Yes, I'm afraid you won't be the first or the last person that this type of thing has happened to,' said DC Bradley, trying desperately hard to say something comforting.

'We probably still have his mobile number somewhere. I can get it for you if you like. I scribbled it down on my pad in the study,' said Frank Renwick.

'We'll take the number, Mr Renwick, but it's likely to be a pay-as-you-go mobile – and he's probably ditched it by now anyway,' said DC Bradley.

Frank Renwick went upstairs to fetch the mobile number.

'Can I ask you again for a further description of this man, Mrs Renwick? Is there anything else you can tell us about him – anything you can possibly recall?' said DC Hodgson.

'Well, he was aged about 25-30, short haircut, quite well spoken. I think he had a northern accent. Well dressed. Other than that, I can't tell you much about him, I'm afraid.'

'Here we are officer, I've copied it down for you,' said Frank Renwick, handing over a piece of paper to DC Hodgson.

'Thank you, Mr Renwick.'

DC Hodgson continued to write the other details down.

'Right, well, we have everything we need for the time being. If you need to speak to us at any time, or if you remember something else, then here is my business card. We will be in touch to arrange collection of the vehicle. I'm very sorry you are involved in this incident, Mr and Mrs Renwick, and thank you once again for your time.'

DC Hodgson got up to leave.

As they stepped through the front door they could hear Mary Renwick breaking down in tears and being comforted by her husband.

'Come on, Pete – let's go and sample the 80 shilling beer down the road. I need one after that,' said DC Hodgson.

CHAPTER 21

Jeff Reynolds drove over to pick Alan Jackson up from his house in Cheadle. Since Jeff's retirement they hadn't seen much of each other. They had worked well together when Jeff was in the force computer department and both men enjoyed each other's company. They had been out for dinner several times but since Jeff's retirement had somehow lost regular contact.

'So – what's so urgent that we need to meet up in a hurry, Alan! We've gone a couple of years without seeing each other, and suddenly everything is urgent?' he asked as Alan climbed into his sports car.

'I'll tell you about it when we get to the pub. I need a drink first – and you'll need a drink when you hear what I have to say.'

Five minutes later they arrived at the White Lion pub and parked up in the rear car park.

The White Lion was a lovely olde worlde pub built in the 16th Century, and over the years it had retained its charm. It was everything an old pub should be, welcoming and comfortable with plenty of the original period features and a menu to satisfy all tastes. Its setting was beautiful – pretty gardens and a lovely view overlooking the Peak District.

As soon as they had got their drinks and taken a seat in a secluded corner of the pub, Alan told Jeff what had been happening to him over the previous weeks.

'Now, let me get this straight, Alan. You are still under suspension while the force investigates you for allegedly storing and selling pornographic material which was found on your laptop? I'm quite honestly flabbergasted!' exclaimed Jeff, who was finding it difficult to take in.

'Yes, that's right, Jeff. It's been a bloody living nightmare I can tell you.'

'I bet it has. Well, do you have any ideas on how these pornographic images got on there in the first place? I mean did you ever leave your laptop unattended, in work or anywhere?'

'No, it never left the desk in my office at home. I think, somehow, someone has accessed it remotely and downloaded the images. It's the only explanation I can think of. I didn't even know they were on the damn machine until the Hi-Tech crime unit had my laptop and picked them up.'

'Do you have any idea who would do such a thing? I know you've ruffled a few feathers in your time over the years, but I can't imagine you with enemies that would go to those lengths.'

'Do you know, years ago when I was a village bobby, I'm sure there would have been people who would have loved to have had one over on me, but since I've been in IT I don't normally get the chance of meeting the public. I can't think who would stoop this low. To be honest, my first reaction was my ex-wife Audrey, but we have been divorced for three years and surely even she wouldn't go that far?'

'So – where is your laptop at this moment?'

'It is still with the Hi-Tech Crime Unit at the force. I have bought a new one since then. I'm assuming I'll get the old one back at some time, when it's eventually been cleaned up by the force.'

'Ok. This needs some careful planning Alan, but I have an idea on how we can possibly trace whoever it is that is framing you. Do you have a backup of your old laptop from before it was handed in to the police?'

'Yes, of course. I always keep my backups on a portable hard drive.'

'Good. We'll restore this on to your new machine, minus the pornographic images of course, as we don't want a repeat of that lot again. It's a long shot and it could work – but whoever planted these images on your laptop may very well have left his calling card on your hard drive too. In fact he could also have left for himself the opportunity to access your machine at a later date. You know what criminals are like – they just can't resist returning to the scene of the crime.'

'Do you mean he might still try to access it now?'

'Well, he might, and that's where we may be able to trap him. This is what we'll do. We'll create a folder on your desktop, let's say we call it MY PASSWORDS. He will be tempted to look in this folder and this is where I will need to set the bait. I've a good mind to set him a virus but that would be illegal! And I have a better idea for trying to identify him. I will need some time, Alan, to go and create this trap, so leave it with me for now and I should be able to have it ready for you for, say, next week. Whatever you do, keep the passwords that you had before. We want to make it easy for him to get back in, and he will know at least some of your passwords.

'I was thinking of changing all my passwords and the memorable information.'

'In an ideal world you should, of course, but we want him in this case to get access to it again. Whatever you do, however, make sure you do change any passwords you have for online banking. We don't want him accessing your bank accounts.'

'Right, I'll try anything, Jeff. This lot is getting to me, as you can imagine.'

'Yes, I'm sure it is, Alan. Now, come on, drink up and we'll go back to your place and take a look at your new laptop.'

***

DC Hodgson and DC Bradley had returned to their office at Midshire Police and were in discussion with the rest of the Operation Carousel team.

'How did it go, Jack? Was it worth the trip up north? Nice quaint hotel I imagine?' asked Ted mischievously.

'Remind me to book you in a hotel next time, Ted,' snapped DC Bradley, sarcastically.

'It seemed like a nice place on the website, Pete, and it was a bit of a bargain! I thought it was within the force expense allowance,' replied Ted defensively.

'Yeah, a bargain it was all right – and well within the force overnight budget. In fact we could have stayed there for a week and it would have been within the one night allowance. Thankfully it was for only one night, but at least we have a mobile number and a name from the visit,' remarked DC Bradley.

'If I can just intervene on this review of hotels and guest houses, gentlemen. Pete, can you double check the two VIN Chassis numbers – the one on the cloned car and the original – and then get in touch with the hire company and let them know that we have located their stolen vehicle. We also need to arrange for it to be collected from the Renwicks. Ted, can you run this mobile number and name through the system? I'm not sure it is going to give us anything, though,' ordered DC Hodgson, handing over his notepad.

Ted was already logged in and was searching on the sparse information he had just been given. With the new data warehouse the force had recently installed it was easy to make a single search across all the systems. This was so different from the past when officers had to log in and out of each system to search for something.

'No, nothing, nil, nada, zilch – computer says no! Lots of James Smiths, of course, but I'll log it in for future, just in case it arises somewhere else. We'll be automatically alerted by the Triggering run if this is spotted in another system,' said Ted.

'I thought as much. I thought it would be too good to be true,' said DC Hodgson. 'Team, I think it's time for a re-think before DCI Bentley comes storming in here wanting results when he calls in for his weekly review this afternoon.'

'Can I just say something, Jack?' interjected Jean.

'Yes of course, Jean. You know all views are considered in here. What is it?'

'I've been thinking about that vehicle that was hired using Dr Stewart's credit card details. Clearly there is some kind of linked fraud going on here. I can't put my finger on it, but do you think it's worth linking up with DS Holdsworth's card fraud team to see if they can throw anything up? You never know what they may have in their case files. I know their analyst Richard pretty well and I can give him a call and arrange to get together to discuss it.'

'Brilliant, Jean. Yes, that's a good point. Get on to this Richard bloke and see what he can tell us. If you have any trouble with DS Holdsworth, let me know.'

CHAPTER 22

They waited until after midnight when the street lights were automatically switched off by the local authority and all the neighbours had gone to bed.

When everything was quiet they collected all their belongings including the food, furniture, bedding and clothing and, as quietly as possible, loaded everything in to the waiting transit van. The children were now fast asleep and were carried out into the waiting car last of all. When they awoke the following morning they found they not only had a new school to attend but had a lovely new garden to play in.

CHAPTER 23

DS Holdsworth was holding his weekly meeting, where the team would review each incident on a case-by-case investigation. Cases which were not going anywhere would be moved to the Pending file temporarily before they were eventually closed unsolved. New information coming to light, which included any new Card Fraud crimes reported and trends in card offences, would be updated and considered for further investigation. Actions would then be raised by DS Holdsworth to follow up any leads for further information.

'Right then, chaps, listen up. We have had a productive month in detecting offences on ATM crimes. We cleared up ten crimes, made six arrests and to date we have charged three offenders. Let's now consider what has been happening from our analyst's perspective. Richard the floor is yours,' commanded DS Holdsworth.

'Well, Jim,' responded Richard, who had only just got used to the idea of calling his boss by his first name. 'The number of incidents of card theft via ATMs has increased by 20% in our area in the last month, but I've been following up on this report we received from a number of card providers who have seen this bizarre situation where offenders have blitzed the card and then vanished without a trace. We are not talking large numbers of incidents here but certainly large amounts financially. The latest suspected incident reported this morning is a family in the Crewe area who appear to have done exactly that.'

'This is unbelievable! How do they think they can get away with it! DC Watkins, can you go with DC Heath to investigate this latest incident further? See what you can uncover. This could well be part of an organised gang. Richard, can you give DC Watkins and DC Heath the details? Let's see what you can find out about the family.'

'Will do, boss – we are straight on to it,' replied DC Watkins, getting his coat on.

'Right, Richard. What do we have so far?'

Richard handed him a copy of the intelligence log.

'It's not much to go on, but we'll see what we can find. Come on, Clive! We are off to Crewe,' announced DC Watkins to DC Clive Heath as he was almost out of the door.

***

Jeff Reynolds had been working long hours into the night developing the source code which would hopefully track down the offender who was trying to frame Alan Jackson. Jeff had always been a bit of a techno-freak, he didn't mind admitting it. He would spend long hours developing computer software in his spare time for friends and always liked a challenge. Jeff had started in computing in the early 1970s as a mainframe computer operator in the steel industry. Those were the days when a computer was the size of a house and had to be accommodated in a fully air-conditioned environment. He'd progressed soon to a shift-leader in the operations room and then quickly into programming when it was discovered that he'd been tinkering with the scheduling of the mainframe computer. The result of this was that on his shift the workload finished far earlier than the other shifts. The operating system support staff spotted this and recommended him for promotion out of harm's way and he was rapidly sent upstairs to the programming department. He'd worked for the police service on systems support before retiring early in the summer of 2014.

That should do it, he thought, standing back and admiring his handy work. If he's curious, I would bet money that he will fall into the trap.

He logged off, packed up the laptop and contacted Alan to arrange to meet up again at the White Lion that afternoon.

***

'There's no answer, John. I've tried looking around the back just in case they are in, I've peered through the windows and the place is deserted. The rooms are empty, there isn't a stick of furniture in the place,' said DC Heath, still peering through the front window.

'Yes, it certainly looks like that,' replied DC Watkins. 'Well, let's try the neighbours to see if they can throw any light on the people who were living here. They might have been told where they have moved to.'

DC Watkins and DC Heath went up the steps and knocked at the house next door. They knew someone was in as they could hear the television blaring loudly. After several knocks they could hear a series of locks and chains being unbolted and eventually an eccentric old lady appeared at the door brandishing a walking stick. Before they had chance to introduce themselves to her she shouted, 'I'm not interested, I'm not expecting visitors, if you've come to sell me double glazing, solar panels or even a copy of the Watchtower, I'm not bloody well interested. All right? So, be off with you before I call the police!'

'But we are police officers, madam. We just need to ask you a few questions, if that's all right?'

DC Watkins had to raise his voice to be heard over the television noise.

'I haven't done anything wrong. I hardly ever go out,' snapped the old lady. 'And anyway, how do I know you're police officers? You haven't got uniforms! You could be anybody!'

'Yes, it's nothing to worry about, madam. We are detectives and it won't take a minute,' reassured DC Heath, showing his warrant card and getting his notebook out. 'Firstly, may I ask you your name? Is it Mrs?'

'Yes, it's Mrs Morris, Elsie Morris, Mrs Morris to you,' she said sharply.

'Did you have any dealings with your next door neighbours, Mrs Morris?' enquired DC Heath.

'Well, no, not really. They kept themselves to themselves. I used to see the three children playing in the garden. They were nice kids, very well behaved. Now and again the ball they were playing with would be kicked over my fence and I'd throw it back to them but they didn't bother me and I certainly didn't bother them. I have no idea of their names or where they were from. They hadn't been living there long – I'd say about six months maximum. Yes, it must have been six months as old Mr Millington from across the road died the previous week and the hearse couldn't get through because they had a big van blocking the road. Yes, six months. He hadn't been very well, you know. He once told me that he had…' replied Mrs Morris.

'Are you aware that they have now moved out?' interrupted DC Watkins.

'Really? No. I thought it was quieter than normal, but, no, I had no idea.'

DC Watkins thought, 'I'd move out if my neighbours had their telly on that loud.'

'When was the last time you saw them then, Mrs Morris?' asked DC Heath.

'Now, let me think. That would be over a week ago. I was pegging out the washing and the children were playing football. It would be, let me think, yes, last Monday. It was definitely Monday as that's my washing day, always will be and always has been. Do you know…'

'And did they say that they would be moving soon?' interrupted DC Heath, not wanting to hear a life history story.

'No. As I say, they were very quiet. They didn't know my name and I don't know theirs.'

'They were Mr and Mrs Kolowski and they are Polish – or so we understand,' piped up DC Watkins.

'Really, now that does surprise me! Ee, fancy! They didn't seem Polish! In fact they all spoke very good English and I thought they had Lancashire accents! I wonder whereabouts from…'

'Thank you, Mrs Morris, you've been most helpful,' said DC Watkins, cutting her short as they returned to their car.

***

Jeff Reynolds and Alan Jackson had met up for lunch and were sitting in the snug of the White Lion pub on their own, well away from the many diners in the main bar.

'Now then, Jeff, so what have you come up with?' said Alan, enthusiastically.

'Well, here is your laptop back and it's already set up. You can continue to use it as normal but don't, under any circumstances, open the folder on the desktop marked MY PASSWORDS. I feel certain that whoever is behind all this will revisit the laptop from time to time and they will be intrigued as to what is being held in that folder. When they open it a routine will be silently downloaded onto their own device which hopefully will be a laptop. When they reboot their own machine the device will automatically take a photograph without them knowing and save the image on their device and, once they are online, transmit the image to a private secure website which we will be monitoring. Oh, one more thing, always leave it switched on and online. Bit obvious but thought I'd better mention that.'

'Ingenious, Jeff! Once we know who the offender is, we can take action without him or her even knowing it.'

'Exactly! Well, it's not quite ingenious, Alan. It will only work of course if, a) the person revisits your laptop and is curious and b) if he or she is on a modern laptop with an inbuilt camera. Oh, and another thing, I've also embedded a GIS location finder in the download so we will not only have a photograph of them, we also will know where he or she lives. My guess is we shouldn't need to wait too long.'

'Now all we need to do is sit back and wait,' said Alan, looking around. 'Talking about waiting, I wonder where that lunch is that we ordered!'

***

Jean Price and Richard Evans had arranged to meet at her office to discuss the investigation into Dr Stewart's stolen credit card details.

'Hi, Richard! Firstly, many thanks for meeting me. As you know, I'm working on this case that we believe is somehow connected with Dr Giles Stewart's credit card. Our understanding is that his card was used to hire a vehicle from Midshire Car Hire just over a month ago. The vehicle was never returned. Have you managed to identify where or when the card details were stolen?'

'I can't give you an exact date but we believe the card was first used on October 27th. We have a list of transactions that took place since that date, all of which were definitely nothing to do with Giles Stewart. We are looking at the transactions that Mr Stewart definitely made prior to that date with a view to trying to identify from where the details could have been stolen. It looks as though he was using the card primarily for hotel bookings, train fares and filling up with petrol. What I need to do now is to cross check the locations of these against other stolen credit cards and that way we should at least get a list of common outlets. With it being a credit card I don't believe we are looking at an ATM and the guy said he never went online, so that whittles it down somewhat. I think the card details were stolen from a skimming device at a petrol station or possibly a restaurant.'

'That's most useful, Richard. Tell me, was the card used after the Midshire Car Rental booking?'

'Actually, yes. The transactions continued for a few days afterwards, primarily for filling up with petrol.'

'That's interesting. If it was used after the card was presented at Midshire Car Rental then there is a fair chance that it was used by the thieves who stole the hire car. Do you have the times and dates of the actual transactions?'

'Yes, we do indeed – although it is quite possible that these could relate to a later time and date depending on the outlet – but generally they should be the right time and date.'

'Do you have the locations of the petrol stations?' Jean asked eagerly.

'Well, yes and no! A number of garages are owned by central companies, you know – a group of garages – so you can't actually see in which location the transaction took place. But I can tell you that they centre around the Crewe area and in particular Dumfries and Galloway.'

CHAPTER 24

Tim Ridgway was now conducting his illegal skimming business from his penthouse apartment in the city centre. He had a bank of laptops set up in the spare bedroom and he rarely visited the Jelly Bean café these days unless Alan the owner called him with any hardware or software problems for him to deal with. The money was rolling in and he bragged to his many girlfriends that he didn't need to leave his apartment. He never told them how he earned his money and they were all under the impression he was some kind of financial broker or investment banker. Money was now no object and he was splashing out big style. He had a whole new wardrobe of clothes and was no longer the scruffy unkempt individual he'd been whilst working at Midshire Police. Charlie continued to look after the day-to-day business, dealing on the dark web with fellow scammers wishing to rent the skimmers, the data from which was now being electronically transmitted back to Tim's mobile phones.

Tim had everything: fast cars, designer clothes, girlfriends hanging off each arm, but despite this he was at times still the loneliest young man in the country. He often became depressed when thinking over the loss of his parents. He frequently had nightmares with visions of the car crash and would wake up shouting and screaming.

He started to think about the revenge plan he had put in place several weeks ago and wondered whether his old boss, in his view, had finally had his come-uppance. He hadn't seen any news in the press of suspensions or dismissals. He was bored one afternoon and decided to see if he could still access the remote laptop. To his surprise he was able to log in. The silly old fool hadn't even bothered to change his password security. He brought up the remote desktop of Alan Jackson's laptop and he could see the same icons and folders that he had before. But, wait! There was a new folder that he hadn't spotted before named 'MY PASSWORDS.' He clicked on it and it seemed to be encrypted. He tried a few things out but he still couldn't read any of the files within. Just then the phone rang and it was Charlie wanting to meet up, so he quickly logged off and made arrangements to meet him later that evening.

***

'What do you mean, he's gone! Gone where exactly?' spluttered DC Hodgson through his early morning coffee.

'Dumfries and Galloway, Jack,' replied Ted. 'He was so impressed with that guest house you stayed in he decided to take a few days' leave and go up there on his own on a fishing trip. In fact he couldn't wait to get back up there!'

'Dumfries and Galloway! You are joking of course! We've got a case to investigate. It's not April the first, is it Ted?'

'Well, partially joking Jack! He's fishing for clues actually. He has definitely gone up north to follow up on a lead that came in following Jean's meeting with the Card Fraud Team. Apparently there are two garages in the Dumfries area where Giles Stewart's cloned card was used. He contacted the garages involved and he reckons that they have reasonable CCTV footage from both the forecourt and the shop.'

'How does he know that Giles Stewart himself hadn't been up there? He might get all the way up there and find he has had a wasted journey, staring at an image of Dr Stewart?'

'Well, that was easy. The transactions happened after the Midshire Car Rental transaction and while Giles Stewart was in Perth, the Australian one!'

'I wish he'd told me before he set out but, heh, at last we might well have a picture of our guy after this,' grinned DC Hodgson, rubbing his hands gleefully.

***

Peter Owen stepped off the plane at Hong Kong International Airport and hurried through to the immigration desks. His connecting flight had been delayed by several hours at Schiphol airport in Amsterdam and he was now late for his meeting with his tailoring supplier in Kowloon.

He was well ahead of the queue at the immigration hall and he sailed through before the rest of the passengers had caught him up. He proceeded onward into the baggage reclaim hall and didn't have to wait long before his bags were the first to turn up.

He'd lost count of the number of trips he had made over the years to Hong Kong and smiled to himself at how streamlined the arrival at the new airport was now compared with the old Kai Tak airport which was a knuckle ride in itself. Once he'd collected his bags he headed through customs and onto the Airport Express for the fast journey into the centre of Hong Kong. Soon he was checking in at a hotel on Nathan Road in Kowloon. He had hoped to check in at his favourite hotel but an international business convention had booked all the rooms previously months ahead and so scuppered his plans. Instead he had booked into an adjacent hotel which had the same spectacular views of the impressive skyline.

'Good evening, sir, and how may we help you?' asked the clerk on the front desk.

'Good evening. The name is Peter Owen. I'm booked in for five nights. Here is my booking reference.'

He handed over the paperwork from his briefcase.

The clerk keyed in the booking reference on the computer.

'Ah, Mr Owen, how very nice to have you back again and so soon. We have reserved the same room you had last time – on the 11th floor with a wonderful view. I'm sure you'll agree! May I personally welcome you back – and I do hope you enjoy your stay with us again.'

'But I haven't been here to this hotel before,' said Peter, who was now very puzzled. 'I think you must be mistaking me for someone else.'

'No, there is no mistake, Mr Owen. You stayed with us, let's see now, it was just over a week ago. We still have your details on file,' confirmed the clerk as he swivelled the computer screen around for Peter to see.

Peter Owen felt sick. He began to realise that not only had someone been using his credit card but they had also been using his identity.

***

Since he had handed the laptop with the embedded code back to Alan, Jeff Reynolds had been visiting the secure website he had set up every day. Two weeks had elapsed since then and Jeff was beginning to think that the plan to trap whoever it was that had framed Alan Jackson would never get off the ground.

'Perhaps it was a bit ambitious,' he thought. Still, it was worth a few days' coding and definitely worth a try to help Alan Jackson out. He was about to go to bed. He'd stayed up late watching a film but he thought, 'I'll just see if we've had a bite.' He logged back into the website to see if the audit log had recorded any entries and to his amazement there it was: an entry for the 3rd of January at 16.25. He couldn't type fast enough. Were there any entries in the location file, he asked himself. To his surprise this too had a set of GPS coordinates. There was no valid IP address recorded but that didn't matter. He opened the images folder and to his sheer delight there it was: a clear picture of a young man staring back at him.

He picked up the phone immediately and rang Alan Jackson.

'Hi Alan, it's me, I'm sorry to wake you but I...'

'Jeff, do you know what bloody time it is? It's 2.30 am! What the hell do you want at this time of the morning?' grunted Alan, interrupting him.

'I've got something for you, Alan. Our man has fallen into the trap and taken the bait,' declared Jeff excitedly.

'You're joking, Jeff! This is a dream you've been having, surely.'

'No dream Alan, I assure you! He, we now know for definite that it's a he by the way, has fallen into the trap and we have GPS coordinates and his image. He's not somebody I recognise but you may very well know him.'

'Right, first thing in the morning, can you get round to my place, Jeff? At last I might be able to put a final end to this misery.'

DC Bradley arrived in Dumfries after a long and tiring journey through sleet and snow. The weather conditions on the motorway had been horrendous and after a brief coffee break at one of the most delightful service areas at Tebay he'd then been stuck in motorway traffic on the Shap in Cumbria for over an hour because of a serious accident on the northbound carriageway. He was exhausted as he arrived at a very nice hotel overlooking the ruins of 13th Century Torthorwald Castle. This is more like it, he said to himself. Jack doesn't know what he is missing. He checked in at the hotel, which was owned by a Mr and Mrs Macauley, a delightful elderly couple who couldn't do enough for him. After a late lunch at the hotel, washed down with a very nice glass of chardonnay, he made his way to the first of the two petrol stations on the A709. He'd already called ahead and spoken to the garage owners and on arrival they provided him with the DVDs of the CCTV recordings for the date and time of the Giles Stewart credit card transactions. He now had everything he needed but he decided to give PC Urqhart a call on the off chance that he was at Dumfries police station.

'PC Jamie Urqhart speaking. How can I help you?'

'Good afternoon, Jamie. My name is DC Pete Bradley from Midshire Police. I'm not sure if you remember, but we spoke on the phone a while ago regarding the Ford Mondeo that was spotted in Newton Stewart.'

'Ah, yes, I remember. How is the investigation going, Pete?'

'Well, it's progressing, it's slow but progressing. I am actually in the Dumfries area at present and wondered whether I could call in to see you. I have some local CCTV footage which I need to review and I'd appreciate your help just to see if you can possibly identify the driver. You know, it could very well be a local guy?'

'Yes, by all means. I'm in the station now if you want to come down and we can see if we can help at all. I'll make sure we have access to the video studio and I'll get the kettle on.'

DC Bradley thought, 'video studio,' that sounds a bit posh! If it's anything like we have back at Midshire Police it's a TV monitor on someone's spare desk!

DC Bradley drove into the police station car park and managed to find a spot to park. Soon, after chatting with the officer on the front desk about the effects of the UK Government cutbacks, he was with PC Urqhart going through the video footage. It didn't take long to fast-forward to the approximate time just immediately before the transactions. One of the recordings was very poor and you couldn't really identify anything but the other had everything they could have wished for, with footage of the forecourt and the shop.

They found the video frames leading up to the credit card transaction and sure enough there it was – the Ford Mondeo registration JX12YUV driving up to the pump. A young man aged between 25 and 30 got out but he wasn't facing the camera. They switched to the image in the shop and they had a near perfect picture of him paying for the petrol, sandwiches and newspaper with a credit card. It certainly wasn't Giles Stewart – but it was his credit card.

'Do you recognise him, Jamie?' asked Pete earnestly.

'Afraid not, Pete. He's not a local man, certainly not one of our regular offenders. He's probably come from over the border,' responded Jamie, shaking his head.

'Well, it was worth a try,' shrugged Pete as he bundled the DVDs into his briefcase. 'I'll take the footage back to our HQ in the morning and run it through the facial recognition system. But thanks anyway for your help. I'll keep you informed of any developments.'

Pete headed back to his hotel and contacted DC Jack Hodgson on his mobile. The call went directly to Jack's voicemail.

'Jack, we now have an image of the driver of the Mondeo. I should be back with you late morning tomorrow. I plan to get an early start. Oh, and by the way, get the video studio ready,' he joked.

***

Alan Jackson couldn't get back to sleep after Jeff's phone call. He got up, made himself a cup of tea and some toast and sat in his armchair by the fire thinking who on earth it could be who was framing him and determined to make his life a misery. Eventually he dropped off to sleep and awoke suddenly when the milkman arrived just before 8'oclock. He hurriedly raced upstairs to the bathroom, shaved and showered before Jeff arrived with his own laptop, shortly after 9am.

'Good morning, Alan,' remarked Jeff cheerily. 'Now, let me see if you recognise this guy. I've downloaded everything onto here.'

Jeff fired up his laptop and opened the folder he'd created to store the image.

'Well, do you recognise him?'

Alan's mouth dropped in shock.

'Do I recognise him! There's no mistake recognising that bugger! I should have guessed it was him all along.'

'Come on then, don't keep me in suspense! Who on earth is he?'

'That, Jeff, is Tim Ridgway! So it's been him all along! He used to work for me and we had to dismiss him from the force for accessing PNC without authority. I should have thought! I knew he took his dismissal badly but never in a million years did I think he would stoop this low.'

'Well, we also have his location, or at least the location from where he accessed your laptop remotely. It appears to be a very exclusive apartment block in the city centre, I presume you are going straight to the police with this, Alan? This guy has to be stopped.'

'No, I think we need to work out our next steps here. We don't want to rush these things,' he replied, to Jeff's surprise.

'How do you mean, Alan? Surely a quick arrest here would clear everything up and you can get your life back to normal.'

'Well, he's given me untold grief over the past weeks and months and I'd like to do the same to him! I'd first like to know what he's up to at present and what he's doing in an exclusive apartment block, for a start. When he worked for Midshire Police he was living in a grotty flat somewhere and didn't have two pennies to rub together. This guy had nothing, nothing except a very good computing brain. No, we need to carry out some surveillance here. I suggest we start by taking a look at this apartment he's living in. Not a word to anyone! Ok? Are you still with me on this, Jeff?'

'Yes, of course I'm with you Alan! I'm as intrigued as you are as to where he is making his money. Oh, but can I suggest you now please change all your passwords, immediately!'

CHAPTER 25

He drove into the hotel car park and parked his gleaming brand new silver Range Rover Vogue in the far corner away from other cars. He locked the car and took the gravel path to the hotel main entrance. Once inside he made his way through the foyer into the residents' bar and took a seat over by the window. He didn't have to wait long before his two colleagues arrived and joined him for lunch. They ordered oysters and champagne and started planning their next moves.

***

Pete Bradley couldn't wait to get back to the Operation Carousel incident room and he put an early morning call in at 6.30am. He had to miss the full Scottish breakfast from Mrs Macauley and settled for a quick coffee and a croissant on the way out. She had also very kindly provided him with a packed lunch for his journey home.

He arrived back at the incident room mid-morning where DC Hodgson was busy studying a link analysis chart that Jean had created for him. The chart highlighted the connections between their investigation and the credit card fraud team investigation.

'Good morning, team,' announced Pete enthusiastically. 'Would you like to have a look at suspect number one?'

'Yes, I've got the "video studio" ready! It's on my desk over there disguised as a TV monitor,' replied DC Hodgson laughingly.

The team gathered around the video monitor and studied the images from the garage shop.

'Well, that's our man all right,' shouted DC Hodgson, pointing to the screen. 'Good work, Pete. He certainly matches the description that the Renwicks gave us. There's just the small matter now of identifying exactly who he is. Ted, can you run that image through the Force Facial Recognition system? It will be interesting to see if he has any previous. And Pete, can you arrange for a joint investigation meeting with DS Holdsworth? Looking at Jean's link chart here, I think we have quite a bit in common with the card fraud investigation team.'

***

Tim Ridgway was now rolling in it and he was enjoying life to the full. Money from his encrypted skimming devices was pouring in, yet he was getting greedier by the day. He couldn't spend it fast enough – but still he yearned for more. He'd decided to take a holiday in the Far East and at the same time visit his device manufacturer. Charlie had agreed to look after the day-to-day business whilst he was away. He booked a flight from Manchester to Hong Kong, travelling first class. This was to be a working holiday as he had an idea how he could improve the skimming device even further but he needed to check out certain hardware issues with his manufacturer.

After fast-tracking through Manchester Airport and spending a relaxing time preparing for his meeting in the business lounge he was now settled back in his seat 1A. Soon he was sipping a glass of champagne as the A380 climbed to 35,000 feet and he thought how his life had changed dramatically in such a short time. He had never visited the Far East before and he was looking forward to meeting his partner-in-crime.

On arrival after his twelve hour flight to Hong Kong International Airport he was met by his contact for the first time: the 'Ghost Orchid,' a charming young man by the name of Chung Lee, known as Jimmy to his friends. Jimmy was the brains behind the manufacturing of the skimming devices. Soon the pair were en route in Jimmy's luxurious Mercedes S class to a five star hotel in the Kowloon area of Hong Kong.

When they eventually arrived at the hotel, Tim checked in with one of his many cloned credit cards. Tariq had also kindly supplied a matching fraudulent passport in return for a handful of bitcoins just in case the hotel needed to see it. He dropped his bags off in his room and re-joined Jimmy in the hotel bar for a quick drink.

'Well, Tim, welcome to Hong Kong! It is good to meet you after all this time – and may I say business is good between us,' proclaimed Jimmy, 'so I am eager to know what this new idea is of yours that you clearly couldn't discuss on the phone.'

'Well, as you know, Jimmy, the device is working well for us both at present but we still run the risk of being traced, should a device ever get into the wrong hands.'

'Well there's no fear of that is there? I mean, everything is encrypted and we only operate in the dark web,' replied Jimmy.

'Well, true, but I think there are possibly other ways of using the device. I'm thinking of remote access! What if we embed a remote capability where the skimmer communicates with our own laptop? The device would be planted as normal but paired with a mobile or laptop. This means I could sit there all innocently in my car not too far away and have any captured data transmitted to my laptop.'

'What an interesting idea, Tim! Yes, I think that would be possible. I also have some news for you. Very shortly, using 3D printers, we should be able to print our own skimming device! It will keep the cost down and mean even more profit.'

'Incredible,' said Tim. 'I knew 3D printing had come on in leaps and bounds, but I hadn't realised it could produce this type of thing. I look forward to seeing one of those! In the meantime, have a think on how we can embed Bluetooth, as it does take the risk out of it. Come on, drink up! We have some celebrating to do over in Wan Chai. I'm keen to visit some of these bars which I've heard all about.'

***

DS Holdsworth was holding his weekly review with the card fraud investigation team. They had had a strange week with more and more card thefts reported – but very little progress on investigations.

'So, give me that again. The family have moved out of the property but have left a credit card bill of in excess of nine thousand unpaid. But the card was in their name and they had been paying their bills up until this point. And this is just a family who have decided to do a runner, isn't it? Surely it's just a moonlit flit? Probably someone made redundant and has been living life to the full. I suggest you file this one for now but keep the details on the triggering system just on the off chance that they re-offend elsewhere. How did it get reported to us in the first instance?'

'Well, don't you remember, sarge? Richard picked this one up and passed it to us for further investigation. We've had a number of these incidents reported to us by the card providers and this is just the first one we followed up. It came from one of our briefings,' replied DC Watkins.

'Oh – right, I recall it now. I think we should, however, concentrate on the stolen card details, chaps, as we could be wasting precious investigative hours here.'

DS Holdsworth paused for thought.

'Ok, this is what we'll do, Richard. I have had a call from DC Hodgson following your meeting with Jean Price their analyst and they would like to have a meeting with us next Wednesday to discuss any possible connections across the investigations. Clive, can you book the meeting room for 10am next Wednesday? It will be interesting to see if there is any synergy with our investigations.'

CHAPTER 26

Jeff Reynolds and Alan Jackson were in Alan's car which was parked on double yellow lines just around the corner from Tim Ridgway's apartment block. They had a clear view of both entrances to the building without raising any suspicion.

'I hope a traffic warden doesn't turn up, Jeff, as I haven't got my warrant card to show him.'

'It should be ok, Alan. We can drive off quickly if we see one coming.'

'I'll tell you what – it's a pretty damn impressive building. Are you sure he is living there, Jeff? I mean, could he have been using someone else's apartment when he accessed my laptop?'

'I double checked and he is definitely living there. In fact he's on the top floor in the penthouse apartment. He hasn't bought it as far as I'm aware but the rent alone on that place must be in the region of two and a half grand a month.'

'And the rest! How on earth he can afford this place is beyond me,' Alan added, pointing up to the penthouse apartment. 'I mean, he was technically a very capable young lad but even programming doesn't pay this well. He is clearly up to something – you mark my words! Did you find out where he's working?'

'I made a few discreet enquiries and it appears he is also actually claiming jobseekers' allowance!'

'What! He's on bloody benefits! Well, I've heard everything now! Unless the welfare state benefits have gone up significantly under this government he has to be up to no good. I mean – doesn't the Department of Work and Pensions spot this type of thing going on? It's no wonder the country's in a mess,' declared Alan.

'Well, for all I know, Alan, they could have him under investigation themselves and are just waiting for their opportunity to pounce.'

'So much for joined up justice systems,' replied Alan.

Just then, to their complete surprise, the electronically controlled smoked glass doors of the side entrance of the apartment block slid open and out stepped Tim Ridgway, dressed in his familiar hoodie, tee shirt, trainers and jeans. He was carrying a laptop bag over his shoulder.

'That's him!' exclaimed Alan Jackson as he slid down in his seat to avoid being seen.

'Are you sure it's him, Alan?'

'Yes, there's no mistake. It's him all right. He's smartened himself up a bit since I last saw him. He's even had a haircut by the looks of it!'

'Well, this is our chance Alan. I'll follow him from a safe distance. I'll see you at your place later and report back.'

Jeff quietly slipped out of the car and pursued Tim Ridgway at a distance down the Oxford Road, away from the city centre.

***

Tariq Atiq was still working at his father's corner shop most days but any spare time he had was taken up with the programming and creation of cloned cards on the information provided by Tim and Charlie.

Tim had first met Tariq when they were at university together, when they were both on the same Computer Science Degree course, but Tariq had dropped out in later years to run his father's shop when his father became ill. Tim and Tariq had stayed in touch over the years and Tim had persuaded Tariq into getting involved with cloned cards. At first Tariq had resisted, as he didn't want anything to do with it if it was illegal, but Tim had twisted his arm and promised him a share of the proceeds.

Tariq had since invested his own money in a card processing device which, when connected to his laptop, meant he could easily code in the details required. He could use any type of plastic card with a magnetic strip to create a clone – loyalty cards, hotel key cards and so on – but more recently he'd found a back street supplier of reproductive cards which even looked just like the original card.

Business for Tariq had been good in the early days, with Tim and Charlie both providing him with stolen data on a regular basis for him in turn to create the cloned cards. But more recently this had dried up significantly, with Tim and Charlie now preferring to sell the data on to other criminals. They had also now resorted to using the new Bluetooth enabled skimmer themselves to obtain data. This had annoyed Tariq as he'd been kept out of the loop completely and so he had fallen out with them. Tariq had, however, resorted to keeping a number of previously duplicated clone cards – and he was now using these wherever he could.

Little did he realise that this would be his downfall.

***

The small meeting room in the Fraud Unit was standing room only when the Operation Carousel team met with DS Holdsworth's investigation team working on Operation Trident.

DS Holdsworth took charge and chaired the meeting and began by welcoming the Operation Carousel officers.

'Good morning, everyone, and welcome to the heart of Midshire Police's top investigation unit, the jewel in the CID crown,' he remarked jokingly. 'Firstly, it might be helpful if I give you a quick update on where we are with our investigations and afterwards you can share with us what it is you are actually looking for. Hopefully you can also provide us with some useful leads if it appears that there are, in fact, connections.'

He continued to provide a current update on the card fraud incidents that were occurring on their patch and on completion sat back in his chair.

'So, DC Hodgson, if you can now tell us how we can possibly assist you? Presumably some of this is of definite interest to you and your team?'

'Thank you, sarge. Yes, it most definitely is. We are particularly interested in the credit card details belonging to Dr Giles Stewart, which was used to buy petrol in Crewe and the Dumfries areas and also the hire of the Ford Mondeo from Midshire Car Hire. Do you now have a list of all the other fraudulent card transactions relating to this particular card?' requested DC Hodgson.

'Yes, we do. As well as the ones you know about we also have a number of others. It appears that the card has been used in shopping malls – including the Arndale Centre – to buy a number of items – clothing, leisurewear and so on. Richard, can you please give DC Hodgson the list of transactions we have to date?'

'Yes, certainly sarge. It's right up to date,' Richard responded as he handed over a photocopy of the list to DC Hodgson.

'We also have something else you may be interested in, which may or may not be connected with your investigation,' added DS Holdsworth.

'I'm all ears, sarge.'

DC Hodgson sat up.

'Well, as I say, this may or may not be relevant, but as part of our investigation we believe there are in fact multiple copies of the same card doing the rounds,' explained DS Holdsworth.

'What next? Multiple cloned cars – and now multiple cloned cards!' exclaimed DC Hodgson.

'That's easy for you to say,' chuckled DC Bradley, falling about laughing and receiving a groan from DS Holdsworth.

'We believe someone has actually reproduced the cloned card. The reason we believe this to be so is that while looking through the transactions for time, date and location we found that the card was used in Bradford on the 31st October at 18.30 and also in Manchester at that very same date and time. We checked with the merchants and they have confirmed the accuracy of their times and dates. It does appear there are two cards out there with identical details!'

'Well, three actually,' piped up DC Bradley. 'Giles Stewart himself has another one in his wallet.'

***

Jonathan Evans had opened his building materials business earlier that morning. He had received a number of sizeable orders over the past week and had spent all of his time getting them shipped to customers. Jonathan just loved the hands-on approach and, whilst he should have been concentrating on the accounts in the office, he felt more at home with his employees in the warehouse driving the fork-lift.

He had taken over the business from his father, who had started the company back in the 1960s, and built it to what, today, was a thriving online organisation. The company provided everything, from a great choice of DIY and trade standard building materials including insulation, plumbing and heating supplies, with deliveries all over the North West.

One of the recent delivery addresses was to a rundown terraced house on the outskirts of Oldham which, judging by the number of materials they had shipped there, looked to be a complete redevelopment project.

He was just going through the paperwork of the last shipment of a final order of expensive kitchen units to that same address in Oldham when he received a telephone call from one of the leading credit card investigation companies.

'Hello. JE Building Materials. Jonathan Evans speaking. How can I help you?'

'Good morning, Mr Evans. NW Card Fraud Services here. We believe you have had a number of online orders for various building materials to be delivered to an address in Kensington Gardens, Oldham. We understand these goods have been charged to credit cards. Is that correct?'

'Yes, it is – and we have yesterday despatched a large order of kitchen units to that address. What seems to be the problem?'

'Well sir, I'm afraid we believe the card or cards that your customer has used to pay for this are in fact cloned. We have had to block a number of cards.'

'But... looking at our records, we have shipped in excess of £11,000 of materials to that house in the past two weeks.'

'Well I'm sorry, but you are unlikely to see the goods again. I'm afraid that suppliers of building materials are often targeted by fraudsters as the goods can be easily sold on. They have probably used that address as a point of delivery and are now well away with the goods.'

'But will I get compensated? As I say, we shipped a large order there just yesterday. I even have signatures on all the delivery notes.'

'I think it's unlikely, sir. The materials will be long gone now and, although the individuals whose credit cards are stolen will normally be reimbursed by the card provider, this, I'm afraid can often be at the cost of the business. I suggest you report this to the police.'

Jonathan's heart sank as he replaced the receiver and prepared to look up the number for Midshire Police.

***

Jeff Reynolds followed Tim Ridgway down Oxford Road and from a safe distance watched him go into the Jelly Bean café. Tim had gone straight in and sat in a corner. He took his laptop out of his bag, plugged in the ethernet and power cables and switched on. Jeff followed him in and ordered a coffee at the counter before finding a table. He grabbed a copy of the Metro paper from a side table and took a seat in the opposite corner.

Jeff took out his mobile and connected into the free Wi-Fi and, in between glancing at the newspaper, pretended to access his email. He thought it strange that Tim had not ordered anything to drink and had just walked in as if he just owned the place; he clearly appeared to be a regular in there using the facilities. Just as Jeff was taking a mouthful of coffee, Tim's mobile phone rang and he took the call.

With the background noise in the café Jeff had a job to hear what exactly was being said but he could just make out the name "Charlie" and "device" being mentioned several times in the conversation. The aggressive conversation got louder and louder. Whoever it was Tim was talking to, they were having a heated discussion to the point that eventually Tim just switched off his mobile in disgust.

He was just halfway through his coffee when, to Jeff's surprise, Tim immediately got up, closed up his laptop, disconnected it and stamped into the back room marked 'Private' followed by Alan, the café owner.

Jeff decided he'd head back to Alan Jackson's place to give him an update so he drank up and headed to the railway station – but just as he was about to leave the café doorway he was approached by a young man who had been watching his every move from the corner.

CHAPTER 27

DC Hodgson and DS Webster had received a call at short notice from DCI Bentley's secretary, Elizabeth Gilmore, asking them to attend an urgent meeting in his office at 10.30 prompt. They had decided to travel together in DC Hodgson's car across town to force headquarters.

'Have you any idea what this is about, sarge? What can be so urgent that we have been summoned at this short notice? I've got a dental appointment this morning which I've had to cancel.'

They sped through the back streets of the city.

'Don't take this the wrong way, Jack, but if it's what I think it is, then Operation Carousel is being shut down as a closed case. It's certainly no reflection on how you have investigated it,' DS Webster commented gloomily.

'But that's ridiculous, sarge! You are joking, I hope. We are getting so close. Don't you ever get that feeling that we are hot on the heels of these offenders? We just need more time.'

'I wish I could share your enthusiasm, Jack, but you have to be honest. We don't seem to have moved forward very much for over a month and it's becoming more and more difficult to justify having the four of you working on it.'

'Yeah, and I suppose it's not helped that the offenders have gone underground. But at least we can say we are at last keeping the crime figures down!'

'Well, there is that! They may not have gone underground – probably have moved on elsewhere. That's certainly one way of looking at it, I suppose.'

DC Hodgson parked the unmarked police car in the visitors' spot and the two officers got out and walked up the steps to HQ reception.

'Good morning! Can I help you?' said the receptionist, not recognising the officers.

'We are here for a meeting with DCI Bentley. I'm DS Webster,' he responded, showing his warrant card.

'Oh! Right, sir, can you please sign in and take a seat. I'll tell Elizabeth Gilmore, the DCI's secretary, that you have arrived and she will come down and collect you shortly.'

DC Hodgson thought about the retort, 'Don't call me Shortly,' but managed to control himself.

The two officers sat in silence whilst waiting to go upstairs to see the DCI. Just then Elizabeth Gilmore, a very large, domineering sort of lady who clearly wouldn't take any nonsense, came marching into the waiting area.

'DS Webster and DC Hodgson I presume?' she asked in her efficient manner.

'Yes, that's right. I'm DS Webster and this is DC Hodgson.'

He stood up and shook her hand.

'Walk this way, gentlemen. The DCI is expecting you. Thank you for coming over at such short notice.'

DC Hodgson thought twice about commenting on the old joke that if he walked that way he'd need to be using talcum powder.

They made their way up the stairs to the DCI's office. The DCI was sitting behind a large, impressive, antique desk laden with paperwork. There were two other officers in the room whom they didn't recognise.

'Ah, good morning, gentlemen. Do come in. Please sit down and make yourselves comfortable. Can I introduce you to DS Windham and DS Clarkson from the National Crime Agency.'

The two officers sat down on the two remaining chairs in the office and nodded to the two NCA officers.

'Now, I won't beat about the bush,' said the DCI, opening the conversation. 'As you know, I'm not one for mincing my words – and I suppose you are wondering why I've called you over for this meeting at such short notice. Well, it's been decided that the National Crime Agency will, as from today, take over the Operation Carousel investigation. The main reason for this is that other forces in the region have been experiencing similar vehicle theft offences – and it makes sense to tackle it from a regional perspective. I am sure you understand. Now I would like you, DC Hodgson, to hand over everything you have on the cases as from today. I'm sure you will cooperate fully with DS Windham and DS Clarkson.'

'But, if I may say so, sir, we feel we are getting close to identifying the offenders,' said DC Hodgson defensively.

'Well, that may be the case, DC Hodgson, but the NCA will probably have more resources they can throw at this. And of course they do have the advantage of receiving other forces' case data which could identify the offenders.'

DC Hodgson thought it was useless arguing with the DCI so he dropped into silent mode.

'I'll arrange for the team to pull together all the case data and get it to you as soon as possible,' said DS Webster, deciding he didn't want to rock the boat and should speak up.

'Well, that's great. Thank you, DS Webster. I'll arrange for one of our team to call you and make the necessary electronic transfer arrangements,' replied DS Clarkson.

'Well, that's settled then,' declared the DCI cheerily. 'I knew we could sort this one out quickly, and can I take this opportunity to thank you especially, DC Hodgson, for the work you have done to date on the investigation. That will be all for now.'

DC Hodgson and DS Webster got up and left the NCA officers with the DCI. Once outside the office and in the corridor DC Hodgson let rip.

'I'm sorry, sarge, but we did all the leg work and at the eleventh hour they have taken it off us! I'm bloody annoyed to say the least.'

'Yes, I realise that, Jack – you and your team have put a lot of effort into this. In fact I think your investigation could well have driven the offenders out of our area, but we must regroup and move on. How do you feel about transferring across to DS Holdsworth's card fraud team? We are under some pressure over there. It will mean you moving out of Broomfields of course and relocating to Divisional HQ.'

'Well, I think they are actually connected, sarge, so yes, move us across. At least we can add value to their investigations. In the meantime I need a drink. Let's go for a pint?'

***

As soon as Jeff Reynolds had arrived home from the station he picked up his car keys and drove straight round to Alan Jackson's house to give him an update on his findings.

It was a beautiful sunny day without a cloud in the sky and Alan was busy in the front garden doing a spot of weeding as the car pulled up.

'I'm surprised you can even find a weed in that garden of yours, Alan! It's immaculate,' said Jeff as he climbed out of his open-top sports car.

'I must admit Jeff, it's never looked this good – but it's all down to the fact that I've had the time to keep on top of it.'

'So, tell me Jeff, how far have you got?' Alan was quick to ask.

'I know a little more at this stage, Alan, but we will have to work out a plan and I'm not sure you'll want to get involved with what I'm about to tell you.'

'Ok, keep it for when we are inside. I don't want the neighbours to hear,' whispered Alan while gathering his tools together and ushering Jeff down the driveway.

They both made their way in through the side door and sat down in the kitchen and Alan switched on the kettle to make a pot of tea.

'Come on then – out with it, Jeff! You know I'm keen to get my own back on that bugger.'

'Well, I followed Ridgway to an internet café. He had no idea whatsoever that I was following him. Anyway, after about ten minutes he received a phone call from someone called… Charlie, I believe.'

'Charlie? The name Charlie means nothing to me. I don't know anyone of that name.'

Alan Jackson shook his head.

'He appears to be an acquaintance of Ridgway. I couldn't hear the whole conversation as there was far too much background noise in the café, but devices were mentioned several times.'

'Devices! What sort of devices?'

'I don't know, but they were having a row of some sort and almost immediately after the call he packed his laptop up and went with the café owner in to the back room. I waited for a while but I think he may have left through the rear exit. I then decided to leave but, just as I was on my way out, a young lad came over and approached me. He'd been drinking and at first I thought he wanted money. I'm sure I could smell alcohol on his breath. Anyway, I think he may have been observing me from a distance watching Ridgway.'

'Oh god, that's all we need.'

'No, hear me out Alan. I think he has given us the information we needed. He asked me was I interested in making some easy money. I went along with it and said yes I was. He went on to tell me that he has access to an ATM skimming device. You know, card skimming.'

'Good God! He's taking a risk, approaching a complete stranger like that. I'm not sure I want to get involved in this Jeff. It sounds very dodgy.'

'No, I thought you wouldn't – and I don't really, but it could lead us to Ridgway.'

'How do you make that out?'

'Well, the lad mentioned he could get hold of one, so I went along with it and pretended I was interested and I asked him if he could get me one by the end of the week. He said he probably could, but he mentioned that he would have to talk to Tim! Now clearly he slipped up here – I may be wrong and it's a long shot but maybe, just maybe it could be Ridgway. It does seem a bit of a coincidence. Do you agree?'

'Yes, I agree. So, how much is this going to cost us?'

'What do you mean, us?' said Jeff light-heartedly.

'Ok, tell me then – how much will it cost me?'

'It's not cheap, he says he wants £500 to rent it. Now, look, we don't have to use the device – but I do think it will lead us to Ridgway!'

'£500! Did he wear a mask and a striped tee shirt? How on earth do you think it could possibly lead us to him?'

'Well according to him, after the device captures card details, it apparently encrypts the data and transmits it to a mobile phone. If my hunch is right, and it is Ridgway, then we've got him. It looks to me as if our friend Ridgway is getting all his money through illegal card skimming devices.'

'Clever! What will these bloody criminals think of next! But I still don't see how on earth that this is going to help us get to Ridgway.'

'Once I have the device, I think with a little bit of help I can reverse engineer it. It clearly has some form of SIM card embedded in it, probably with a user-definable mobile number, I think I can get at the mobile number from inside it. If I'm right, I think it will connect to one of Ridgway's mobiles.'

'But what if it's a pay and go mobile? We won't be able to pin it down to him?'

'Yes, I've thought of that and it could very well be a pay and go mobile, but that's when you will have to involve Midshire Police. We can give the SPOC (Single Point of Contact) team the mobile number and they will have to obtain the call records from the service provider. If my guess is correct, I think our friend Ridgway will have been using the phone regularly and it will also lead us to his contacts. We should be able to get his contact numbers off the SIM card.'

'The sooner we can get this sorted, the better. Yes, I'll give you the £500. It'll be worth it just to bring this hell to an end. But how are you going to contact the guy you met in the café?'

'Oh, that's easy! We've exchanged mobile numbers! I'll call him when I get home and arrange to meet him. The sooner I can get hold of the device, the sooner I can start looking at it.'

CHAPTER 28

Tim Ridgway sat in his high-powered Mercedes CLA-class coupe parked across the road from the ATM on Highgate Road. Tim was changing his cars on a regular basis. He was listening to his favourite Dire Straits CD tracks whilst his mobile phone was plugged into his hands-free unit. He sat and waited patiently for his first customer. In the early hours of the morning Charlie had been out and planted the skimming device and pin pad on the ATM. It was now mid-morning, the rush-hour had just finished and people were going about their daily business. A smartly dressed young mother pushing a baby in a pram stopped and opened her purse; she took out a debit card to withdraw cash from the ATM. She was on her way to meet with other young mothers at the nearby coffee house. Tim watched her from the comfort of his car as she inserted her debit card into the card slot and entered her pin details into the number pad. He felt no guilt whatsoever – he was past caring what people thought about him. In a few short months he had become rich beyond his wildest dreams but, at the same time, the lowest of the low. To him it had become a habit; the more he did it the more he wanted. It was an addiction to stealing from the innocent unsuspecting public.

Immediately a display of the bank details and the pin number she had entered in the ATM popped up on the screen of Ridgway's mobile phone. He pressed save on the mobile app. It was that easy, he thought to himself. Why bother going to work when I can live like this? The Bluetooth app worked a treat, he thought. He waited for another hour during which he captured six further transactions. He then texted Charlie to come and remove the skimming device and pin pad later that night.

Tim Ridgway had enough for what he wanted and headed back to his apartment; he would later download all the transaction details from his mobile phone onto his laptop. Contrary to belief, the bank details would not be used immediately but held for months and it would be a while before any of the victims would even suspect they had been robbed. He now had them safely stored for his own personal use in the future.

***

DS Webster gathered his small team together in the Operation Carousel meeting room to give them all the bad news.

'Now, listen up guys – I'll give it to you straight, you are not going to like it. As from today, we've been closed down. We just didn't come up with any arrests and whilst the DCI recognises that we have all worked hard on this, he has now agreed to hand over the entire case to the National Crime Agency.'

'The NCA! So does that mean we are all going to be seconded to the NCA? I've always fancied working with them,' Ted replied innocently.

'No, I'm afraid not, Ted,' explained DC Hodgson. 'It does mean we are handing everything over to them but you will be pleased to know that we as a team are, however, sticking together and being relocated to Operation Trident, the card fraud team, who need our assistance. We report to DS Holdsworth at Divisional

HQ. In the meantime can you please archive all the data on the system, and pull together all the supporting documentation from our files and then we can arrange to transfer the data to them.'

'I presume we leave the case data in the system just in case the triggering comes into play,' said Ted. 'Surely we are not going to archive that as well?'

'Yes, of course Ted, as far as I'm concerned it is almost business as usual. I'm convinced the card fraud incidents are connected to the vehicle crimes somehow and I'm pretty sure the triggering system will alert us to some of those connections. By the way, Ted, did the Facial Recognition system bring up any matches from the Scotland CCTV images?' replied DC Hodgson.

'No, nothing Jack – although we have now left the image on the image database, just in case.'

'Pity that. I thought that may have given us a few clues. Ah well, c'est la vie.'

'I'm far from happy about this, Jack. We've put an enormous amount of effort into this investigation so far and, just as I think we are getting close, it's taken from under our noses. It's bloody typical of HQ that someone else gets the glory for our hard work,' proclaimed DC Bradley despondently.

'Yes, I agree with you, Pete. I was also annoyed when I found out but I think there are clear links in the card fraud investigations – and if we can get there before the NCA, so much the better. Remember, they have to familiarise themselves with the case first so they have a steep learning curve. We, on the other hand, have a clear advantage, as we know what we are looking for.'

DC Hodgson hoped he was reassuring his team.

***

Tariq Atiq had opened up the corner shop early that morning to get ready for the arrival of the daily newspapers. He'd been up all night in any case as he couldn't sleep for thinking about how Tim Ridgway and Charlie Ellis had done the dirty on him by walking away from their business arrangement. As the days went by Tariq became more and more bitter. After all he had invested a lot of his time and money into the card replication device, only for it to end up on the shelf. Ridgway was now no longer interested in producing cards: instead he just used or sold the bank details he was illegally obtaining. Whilst they were just about on speaking terms they had had a huge argument and their relationship would never be quite the same again. Tariq had also got quite used to the level of income he had been earning from the scam and he was determined to run his own thing now by also stealing identities and buying and renting Ridgway's skimming devices. Tim saw this as a consolation gesture to Tariq. It was something that Charlie was far from happy with and he didn't trust Tariq one little bit.

Tariq was just dealing with a customer who was wishing to buy the morning newspaper and cigarettes when he took a call on his mobile phone.

'I met you in the internet café the other day. I'm interested in renting that device you mentioned. It seems an easy way of making money,' said the voice on the other end.

'Oh, right. Yes, I remember you. I can arrange that for you. As agreed, it'll cost you £500 to rent it for, say, six weeks and I do need the money in cash beforehand.'

'Well, I'm prepared to give you £250 up front, and the rest when you deliver the device. Bring something with you of value for me to keep as security in case you decide to do a runner with my money! By the way, I don't even know your name?'

'Ok, that will be fine. The name is Suma,' said Tariq, not wishing to give out his real name. 'It's a deal. Meet me at the Jelly Bean café tonight at eight o'clock. I'll see you then.'

Tariq finished the phone call and couldn't help noticing that the customer, who was still waiting for his shopping to be recorded on the till, had clearly been eavesdropping on the conversation.

'Just renting my old flat,' said Tariq casually as he swiped the bar codes on the till.

CHAPTER 29

DC Hodgson and his team had boxed up all their belongings: computers, printers and filing cabinets had all been collected by the support staff and were now en route in the removal van to the Card Fraud Investigation offices. The place looked deserted and was now ready for one of the MIT Holmes incident units to move into.

All the data from the investigation had been electronically transferred to the National Crime Agency and archived, together with all the supporting documentation, including witness statements, actions and officers' reports.

Ted and Jean had gone on ahead to claim their desks in the new office at Divisional HQ in readiness, but DC Hodgson and DC Bradley were left behind, having one last final check.

'Well, that's it, Jack. It's time to move up to divisional HQ. I enjoyed working down here. It was nice and quiet with no disturbances but there's nothing more we can do,' murmured Pete, getting his coat on.

'You're right, Pete, but cheer up and look at the time! They're open! Let's go and have a final lunch time pint at that nice little local before we head up the road.'

'Good thinking Jack! Come on, it must definitely be your round!' replied Pete as he unpinned the Operation Carousel sign and closed the door at Broomfields for the last time.

***

Jeff Reynolds caught the packed train into Manchester that evening and made his way down the Oxford Road to the Jelly Bean café. Jeff, who was normally smartly but casually dressed, didn't want to look conspicuous so had dressed down in leather jacket, tee shirt, jeans and trainers. He was going to go into the city a little earlier and have a pint or two beforehand but decided it would be best to keep a clear head and go straight to the café. He walked into the café rather nervously, thinking he may be walking into some sort of a trap. He ordered a flat white coffee and took a seat in the corner. The café was virtually empty apart from a couple of university students who were busy chatting. Just then, almost on the hour, Tariq walked in with a small package under his arm.

'Are you Jeff, the chap who rang me earlier this morning?' enquired Tariq, who had clearly forgotten what Jeff even looked like.

'I am indeed. You must be Suma,' replied Jeff, getting up to shake his hand.

'Yes – but before I hand over the item of security, which incidentally is my gold wristwatch that my dad gave me, have you got the money with you?'

'Of course. Here it is,' whispered Jeff, showing him briefly a brown envelope from inside his jacket pocket.

They exchanged the envelope and package under the table.

'So when will I get the goods?' enquired Jeff, thinking have I just paid £250 for a duff watch.

'I should have it by Friday this week. I suggest we meet here Friday at 9.30am when the café is likely to be pretty much empty. If there is any change to that I'll let you know. And, by the way, bring my watch back when you come,' responded Tariq as he quickly left the café.

CHAPTER 30

Charlie Ellis had received a phone call from Tim, asking him to drop off one of the encrypted skimming devices and associated pin pad at Tariq's corner shop. At first Charlie had refused and told Tim point blank that he wasn't his lackey and asked how did they know where the skimming device would finally end up once Tariq had got his hands on it? Clearly he really didn't trust Tariq one bit and the recent arguments between the three of them had taken its toll on their relationships. Tim informed him that he alone now held the stocks of devices and they had no real control anyway of who bought or rented the device. Even when people bought the devices through the dark web it was a risk they would have to take.

Charlie eventually caved in and reluctantly called round to Tariq's shop to deliver the device and pin pad.

When he arrived Tariq was busy serving a number of customers so Charlie pretended to browse through the magazine shelf above the daily newspapers. Five minutes later, when the last customer had finally gone, Tariq came over and put up the closed sign and locked the door.

'Hi Charlie,' said Tariq. 'Have you got the device?'

'Yes, but be careful, Tariq – we don't want this to end up in the wrong hands,' replied Charlie, handing over the package. 'Who is it for anyway? Is it for you?'

'Oh, just a friend of mine. No-one you know. Look, it's not a problem – he's renting it from me. I'll give you the £350 later.'

'Can you trust him, though? We don't want this finding its way into the wrong hands.'

'Oh yes. I can trust him, no fear there,' replied Tariq, who clearly was so desperate for money that he was unsure who the person actually was.

'Well, just make sure it gets returned to us, ok? And on time!'

'Will do, Charlie – and in any case you'll get a batch of new card details from the rental so you'll do all right out of it.'

'Well, yes, there is that. Look, you've got it for six weeks maximum, ok?' said Charlie, as he unlocked the door and left the shop.

***

DS Holdsworth was chairing the first meeting of his newly-expanded team in the divisional HQ conference room.

'Good morning, everyone – and a special welcome to DC Hodgson, DC Bradley, Jean and Ted. You are very welcome to join the team and your help will be much appreciated in our investigations. I feel sure that you will get on well with everyone. Clearly you probably still have your minds on car thefts but can I remind you that the emphasis here is firmly on credit and debit card fraud. I am sure you will fit in well with the team and may I say how lucky I am to have not just one but two crime analysts working with us. As you know, we have seen a significant increase in card theft in the past few months and I don't need to remind you that fraud comes in many forms, and it's not always obvious that the theft has actually occurred! You'll see what I mean by that statement in a moment.'

'So, how do you see the team carving up the investigation work, sarge? We clearly don't wish to disrupt your current setup,' asked DC Hodgson, who was eager to get started but at the same time wanted to tread carefully.

'Jack, for the time being I propose that your team will take all enquiries relating to identity fraud and these so-called phantom card holders. My team will take the reports of ATM and cheque fraud. Clearly both enquiry teams will report to me. There will be a crossover but that's inevitable. Is that clearly understood?'

'Yes, understood, sarge, but what exactly do you mean by phantom card holders?' asked DC Hodgson, who was clearly puzzled by the term.

'Well, Jack, these are instances of situations where the card is in fact completely legitimate but we believe it has been used by another person or persons connected with the card holder. They are normally new card holders who pay off the amounts each month in full at first and gradually build up a bigger credit limit, then after a few months they hit the card hard and do a runner from the address of the card holder. The incidents have been reported by the card companies when they have been monitoring the change in spending patterns and of course when they fail to pay the balance. The difficulty we have with this, of course, is that by the time the card company report it to us, the offenders are well and truly gone.'

'Fascinating. But surely they have other addresses that these people are using?'

'Yes, that appears to be part of the scam, they actually take on new addresses – and new identities, we suspect – and they even pay the mortgage for a few months before they disappear without trace. They use false documents to obtain mortgages and target houses to buy which are ready to move into. We think it is an Eastern European organised gang, possibly from Poland or Romania, but we are on to them and that's where you and your team will help us enormously. I suggest you speak with DC Watkins and DC Heath who can brief you and provide you with more information.'

'Right then – let's get started! What are we waiting for?'

DC Hodgson turned to DC Bradley.

'Are you thinking what I'm thinking, Pete?'

'Too right! I'm thinking, back to that interview with that lockup garage owner.'

***

Jeff Reynolds took the train into the city on that Friday morning. It was as busy as ever with commuters having to stand for most of the journey. Jeff turned up as arranged at the Jelly Bean café right on time. Tariq (or Suma as he was known to Jeff) was already sitting there waiting patiently in the corner. As predicted the café was empty apart from Tariq and the owner, Alan, who was tidying the place up after the night before.

Jeff pushed open the door, nodded across to Suma, ordered himself an expresso coffee and took it over to his table.

'Good morning, Suma. I trust you have the goods?' Jeff spoke in a whisper and pulled up a chair.

'I do, indeed, but first – do you have the money and, of course, my watch?'

'Certainly,' replied Jeff, flashing a brown envelope from inside his leather jacket and removing Tariq's watch from his wrist.

Both men then exchanged envelope and package under the table. Jeff pushed the watch over to Tariq. Jeff couldn't help noticing that the owner of the café was trying to listen in on the conversation. Anyone watching would have thought Jeff had just sold him a dodgy replica watch.

'I presume there are some basic instructions with this?' whispered Jeff, taking a quick peek in the package.

'Yes, everything is there. It's pretty straight-forward. You shouldn't have a problem with it. It's all there, including how you obtain the decrypted data that you capture, but you can call me if in any doubt. You have six weeks to use this and then I want it back pronto or you'll have to pay for further weeks' rent. Is that understood?'

'Understood. So, who is it that decrypts the data?' enquired Jeff, slyly, clearly trying to catch him out.

'You don't need to know that. It will be done automatically and I will give you the list of decrypted data,' murmured Tariq. 'All you have to do is plant the device at an ATM with the pin pad and sit back and wait. I suggest you do this either late at night or very early in the morning whilst no one is about. Naturally you won't be able to run off with the device as you won't have access to the encrypted data, so don't even think about it. Oh, and another thing, if you want a physical clone of any cards then I'm your man! Ok?'

'What? Do you mean you can actually reproduce the cards?'

'Yes, of course I can – but we can discuss that the next time we meet. Just one thing at a time for now.'

'I quite understand,' responded Jeff, who had no intention of going anywhere near an ATM with it or for that matter cloning any cards.

'Six weeks ok?'

'Yes, no problem. I'll be in touch nearer the time,' confirmed Jeff [thinking, or at least the police will, if we act fast enough].

Jeff finished his coffee and left the café, leaving Tariq counting his money under the table, and made his way back to Piccadilly station. He had already arranged for a former colleague to meet him over at his house in the afternoon to start work on reverse engineering the device.

CHAPTER 31

DC Hodgson was holding his first meeting as part of the Operation Trident card fraud team; he had asked DC Watkins and DC Heath to join them as he wanted a formal handover and wished to know more about the phantom card incidents.

'Right, come on then, let's get started! Good morning everyone and thank you to DC Watkins and DC Heath for joining us today to help with the handover. Can I start the ball rolling? Clearly we are interested in the circumstances around these so-called phantom card incidents as we believe they are linked with other activities and they could very well help us with other enquiries – so can you please present to the team this morning what you know so far?'

DC Watkins was the first to speak and, looking through his notes, said, 'Thanks Jack. Well, it's like this. All we can tell you is that in following up the address of one of the latest incidents we were expecting to find a Polish family living there. The terraced house in Crewe was mortgaged to a Mr Wojek Kolowski, who we believed to have recently moved there from Warsaw. Apparently he is working on a building site in Crewe but to date we have not been able to trace him or the building site.'

This resulted in some light-hearted banter amongst the team.

'Anyway, they had put down a small deposit and seemed to be a genuine family, according to the bank who had loaned them the money. In fact the bank manager told us that Mr Kolowski was a most charming and polite man. When we got there they had completely disappeared and at this stage we haven't yet traced them.'

'But this means that whoever it is that is paying a deposit down on the house loses it when they do a runner?' interrupted DC Bradley.

'That's right, Pete – but our guess is that they don't care because it's a small deposit and the money they are putting down doesn't belong to them anyway. They've probably stolen it from some other scam. The property is just a means to an end as it enables them to have somewhere as a base but, more importantly, to build up for a big credit card fraud,' interjected DC Heath.

'Anyway – when we arrived at the address the house was empty. Nobody had seen them leave or, for that matter, knew that they were going, and when we spoke to a couple of their neighbours they believed the family of five, by their accents, were not Polish but were in fact from Lancashire,' DC Watkins continued. 'It's a bit of a mystery really as, whilst they were there, they paid the mortgage as normal for several months. Again it was probably stolen money and they were given credit cards after a couple of months. They even paid the balances off each month for a while – but left an unpaid debt of £9,500. We have no idea where they have moved to. We think they are possibly still in the area, maybe around Crewe or possibly in the Potteries in the Stoke-on-Trent area but that's as far as we have got on this one. It's just a hunch, but we think they have been doing this type of thing for some time, buying a house and moving out after a few months,' said DC Heath.

'But we definitely know it's a family of five?' enquired DC Bradley, who was busy making notes.

'Yes, we believe they have three children but we have no idea at this stage as to their ages.'

'Do we have the complete records of all the credit card transactions or can we at least obtain them?' asked Jean.

'Yes, we do have them. Richard can provide you with those but why would you want to see them?' asked DC Watkins.

'Well, it's a long shot but we might just be able to work out the ages of the children if they have been buying clothes or shoes, for example, on the cards,' replied Jean.

'Good thinking, Jean! Yes, see if you can work out a profile of this family. Let's leave it at that for the time being. Pete and I will speak to the estate agents around Crewe and the Potteries area to see if they can offer anything on enquiries that they may have had recently. Ted, can you index what comes back from this? I'll raise the appropriate actions and I suggest we meet up again on Friday afternoon to review everything we have so far. In the meantime, thank you, DC Watkins and DC Heath, for spending time with the handover. It is very much appreciated. I just have one more announcement to make before we get back to the job in hand, which is that DC Heath will be joining us as from today. So, welcome on board, Clive. I am sure your knowledge of these incidents will prove invaluable to us and if you can work with Jean on the credit card statement transactions that would be a great help.'

***

***

Jeff Reynolds and his ex-colleague Joe Smithson were at Jeff's home, examining the skimming device and the pin pad overlay. Joe had worked with Jeff in the past at Midshire Police, primarily on server support. He was originally a hardware engineer who serviced the force computer mainframes but had since moved on to become a specialist in mobile technology, particularly in the development of apps.

'So, this is it then, Jeff,' said Joe, as he carefully prised the back off the skimming device. 'Somewhat basic, isn't it, so you paid £500 for this? And this one looks as if it's powered by three AAA batteries.'

'£500 just to hire it!' remarked Jeff.

'This is so basic! Some of these components are made up from parts which appear to have been cannibalised from an old MP3 player or something similar, possibly an old mobile phone,' remarked Joe,

180

continuing to dismantle the various parts making up the device.

'Well, it communicates somehow, Joe, through texting any captured data,' said Jeff. 'I'm not an expert but I guess there must be some sort of SIM card embedded in there.'

'There is indeed, Jeff, and here it is!' He removed the micro SIM card. 'I think this is what you're looking for. This little beauty means that this skimming device would actually allow the thief to receive any stolen card data from almost anywhere in the world, provided they have a working mobile phone signal.'

'Brilliant, Joe! I've got an old mobile here. Let's see if we can download the contacts onto it. It should be charged up.'

Jeff slotted the SIM card into his old phone and switched it on. There was no pin number or password set-up and he copied the contents and then looked inside the contacts folder.

'Just as I suspected, Joe, there are a number of entries here: charlie, home, tariq, this no, something called xmit. They are all mobile numbers but there is also one called 'ghost' at an international number prefixed 852, wherever that is,' said Jeff, scrolling down the list and making a note of all the numbers. 'At some time he's also been using this same SIM card to make calls from his mobile by the looks of it. I'll pass these onto Alan, who will now have no option but to involve Midshire Police, as they can obtain the actual call records for this phone.'

'D' you know, I would love to ring some of these numbers to see who in fact answers but I think it's best waiting for the police to do their thing,' added Jeff excitedly.

'Yeah, we certainly don't want to alert them and frighten them off.'

Joe reassembled the skimming device and handed it all back to Jeff, who packaged it up again.

'Thanks again, Joe, for your help on this. I owe you one.'

'No problem, Jeff. Any time. Just let me know how you get on. I'm sure you are on the right track here.'

Joe smiled as he left the house.

Jeff sat down and made a series of notes ready for his next meeting with Alan.

CHAPTER 32

Jean Price and DC Heath had been working through the bank transactions on the Wojek Kolowski credit card. They had spent time, with the co-operation of the bank, chasing the counterfoils where the transactions had taken place. Most transactions had been on visits to two shopping areas, the Arndale Centre in Manchester and the Potteries' centre in Hanley, Stoke-on-Trent. There were some petrol transactions but the majority appeared to have been for clothing – children's clothing in fact – and there were a couple of slips from fast food restaurants.

Jean was just starting to create a timeline of the dates and times of the clothing transactions when DC Hodgson and DC Bradley returned from their calls and visits to various estate agents in the area.

'Well, that seems to have been another complete waste of time,' moaned DC Bradley in a temper, throwing his jacket onto his chair. 'It was like getting blood out of a stone. Even when I showed them my warrant card they couldn't give me what we wanted. If you ask me, it was a complete waste of time and effort.'

'Not necessarily, Pete. I think we have whittled it down to an area at least,' said DC Hodgson defensively.

'A bloody big area, Jack, and there appear to have been multiple occurrences of Polish or people with

Lancashire accents enquiring about houses – and probably the vast majority are genuine.'

'Yeah, but you know how it is – we had to check it out, Pete. It's a case of joining the dots. I agree in isolation some of this data might seem completely worthless but when you connect them that's when the big picture emerges. Ted, can you index the visit reports from these?'

DC Hodgson handed him a pile of papers, not wishing to be side tracked by Pete, who had clearly got out of the wrong side of the bed.

'Will do, boss. That should keep me busy for a while,' replied Ted, adding them to his already expanding filing tray.

'Anyway... Jean, how have you and Clive got on?'

DC Hodgson now wished to change the subject, albeit slightly.

'Not too bad, Jack. I think we are definitely looking at a family with three children and the ages are five, seven and nine. Looking at the transactions and what they have actually purchased I think it must be two girls and a boy, the boy being the youngest. We've loaded the transaction data into the Link Analysis database and we can show you a timeline of the transactions.'

Jean's enthusiasm was clear.

'That's brilliant, Jean. I'm glad someone round here is making progress. At last we might be getting somewhere! Well done, both of you.'

'But there's something else you should know, Jack,' responded DC Heath excitedly. 'We plotted all the transactions on where the goods were bought including the petrol stations they had used and we can now show you on a map the geographic area we are looking at. In fact we can plot the movement of each of these. We think they are still in the area.'

'Bloody fantastic! D'you know what we've got to do next, Pete?' said DC Hodgson, hoping to cheer him up.

'Go on, surprise me,' grouched DC Bradley, trying to show some enthusiasm.

'Well, these three children presumably must attend school somewhere. Do you agree?'

'Agreed.'

'And they will have probably moved school recently, so we, Pete, are going to call the junior schools in that area to see if they have had a new family with three children in that age group moving in part way through the term, I mean, there can't be many of those, can there?'

'Ted, can you draw up a list of primary schools in that area? I think we could be on to something here!'

***

Jeff Reynolds decided that he now had sufficient information for Alan Jackson to pass the details on to Midshire Police. There was only a certain amount of investigation work that Alan and Jeff could do on their own and their investigation now needed the power, authority and backing of Midshire Police to follow up on what they had uncovered so far. Jeff headed over to see Alan as soon as Joe had left.

'Break it to me gently, Jeff,' groaned Alan Jackson as he opened the front door to him.

'Wait till you see what I've got!' replied Jeff breathlessly.

'Great! How have you got on? I didn't think this would lead us anywhere and would be money down the drain, my money!'

'I think we've got him, Alan – him and his associates!'

Jeff stepped inside the hallway.

'At last, I knew you were the man to help me in sorting out this mess.'

'Well, we are not quite there yet, Alan – but wait till I show you this.'

Jeff and Alan sat down at the dining-room table and Jeff placed the package on the table. He opened up his notebook to the page of scribbled names and phone numbers.

'Well, that's where your £500 went, Alan. It's not much to look at I'm afraid,' said Jeff, opening the package, 'but I think you'll find in the long run it will have been worth it. We've opened it up and extracted the SIM card that it would be using to text the captured card data to other mobiles. In examining the SIM card contents we have also found the following details, names and phone numbers.'

Jeff ripped out the list of details from his notebook and handed it to Alan.

'Here, Alan – these are the details we've managed to extract from the SIM card. Do any of these look familiar?'

'Is Ridgway's number on here?' asked Alan glancing down the list.

'Well it could be. I don't know, but these will need checking out. Do any of the names or numbers here ring a bell?'

'No, none, they mean nothing whatsoever to me.'

'We need to check that out and you will need to share this now with Midshire Police, as soon as possible. They will have to obtain the call records from the service provider but I'm pretty sure this will lead you back to him. I think the phone number for the xmit entry is transmit which will lead you to Ridgway and, as I said before, the number for the SIM card phone is likely to be a pay-as-you go. The other numbers are probably his associates and I've checked the international one which is a Hong Kong number. It's just a guess but I think that number leads us to whoever supplied the skimming device in the first place.'

'Thanks, Jeff, this is really good news! And, as you say, I think our next step has to be with the involvement of the Midshire force. We can only do so much on our own.'

'I'm glad you agree. I feel sure they will listen to you when you give them this information. When will you call them?'

'I'll give Chief Inspector Newton a ring now and ask him to come over. I'll be glad when this is over and I can finally get back to work. At last it looks like the end is in sight.'

***

Jack and Pete had made arrangements to visit a primary school in the South Cheshire and North Staffordshire area. They were now en-route through Congleton heading down the A527 towards Biddulph. The two officers had already made several phone calls to a number of schools in the area to ascertain whether any of them had received three new pupils from the same family part way through the school term. Most drew a blank and had resulted in no further action but one in particular had yielded a result. Without wishing to go into detail on the telephone or even alerting the pupils DC Hodgson had decided to visit the Head Teacher of the school in question.

'According to the sat-nav, Pete, it should be signposted along here, just on the right hand side,' remarked Jack, who was navigating from the passenger seat.

Just then, sure enough there it was, a turning down a single track lane signposted Bridgwater Primary School. As they turned a sharp bend the school came into sight – a delightful stone-built building which looked as though at some time it could have been a village hall. A really good example of a proper, good, old-fashioned village school. You could almost imagine the crates of small milk bottles stacked outside the porch in days gone by. Pete parked the car on the side road and they made their way through the iron gates across the playground and entered through an ivy clad porch to the right of the building.

'Good afternoon. Can I help you?' said the receptionist, opening the sliding hatchway.

'Yes. Good afternoon. We are DC Hodgson and DC Bradley from Midshire Police and we have an appointment with Mrs Ramsbottom,' replied DC Hodgson, showing his warrant card.

'Ah, yes, Mrs Ramsbottom said you were coming. Can you please sign in. I'll tell her you are here. Please take a seat while you are waiting.'

The receptionist pressed a button under her desk and the old oak door creaked and clicked open. The two officers signed the visitors' book and went in and sat on the two waiting room chairs in the corridor.

A few minutes later Mrs Ramsbottom, a very well-spoken lady in her late fifties, arrived carrying a document under her arm.

'Good afternoon, officers, and welcome to Bridgwater Primary School. Please follow me into my study and you can tell me how we may be able to help you.'

The two officers followed her down a well-lit corridor which had a number of wall coat hooks part way down the wall, all laden with coats and satchels.

DC Hodgson couldn't help but notice that there were individual photographs of each pupil above each coat hook and he thought how things were so much different now to when he was in primary school. There would be duffle bags and old leather satchels but today there was a complete range of Thomas the Tank, Spiderman and Bart Simpson bags on show.

They turned right into the small book-lined study and took a seat.

'So, gentlemen, how can we help you? I trust there is nothing wrong?' said Mrs Ramsbottom, forgetting at times she was talking to two plain clothes officers.

'No, Mrs Ramsbottom, nothing to concern yourself, but, further to our phone call this morning... you mentioned that you have recently received three new pupils part way through the school term from the same family? We believe the ages are five, seven and nine?' replied DC Hodgson.

'Yes, that's correct, officer, the Robinson family. They are delightful children. The family moved to the area recently apparently. The children's names are Daniel, Emily and Lucy. They joined the school about six weeks ago.'

Mrs Ramsbottom consulted her documents.

'Do you have a previous address for them?' asked DC Bradley, who was making notes.

'No, I'm afraid I don't unfortunately. I understand they were living with their grandparents in Bolton before moving here.'

'And I assume you do have their new address now, of course?'

'Oh yes, I have it here. They live in 48 Westpool Terrace, Biddulph. Are you quite sure there is nothing wrong, officer? Would you like me to call them from their lessons?'

'No, nothing to worry about, Mrs Ramsbottom, and please do not inform them of our visit. We don't wish to disturb them. We are just following a few enquiries and are checking out one or two things.'

DC Bradley thought about asking if they had Polish accents but decided he had better not embarrass himself.

'Well, thank you, Mrs Ramsbottom. That will be all. You have been most helpful.'

'Not at all. Please let me know if we can be of further assistance. I'll just show you back to reception.'

On the drive back to the office Pete asked, 'Do you think this is really the family we are looking for? They don't sound very Polish, do they? I'm beginning to think that with a name like Robinson and the fact that they have been living with their grandparents these are not the family from Crewe we are looking for.'

'I'm not so sure, Pete, but we will need to visit 48 Westpool Terrace and find out a bit more about Mr and Mrs Robinson. In the meantime I spotted a nice little tavern on the way back and, as you are driving, I won't be on shandy! In fact, I can already taste the first pint!'

CHAPTER 33

Alan Jackson had arranged for Chief Inspector Newton to come over to his house. He had informed him on the telephone that he now had fresh evidence relating to his case which they needed to look at as soon as possible.

'Good morning, Chief Inspector. Thank you for coming over so soon. Please do come in.'

'Good morning, sir,' responded the Chief Inspector, still wishing to maintain the courtesy of speaking to a senior officer.

They went into the lounge and sat down.

'Now then, sir, you mentioned on the phone that you have some new evidence that we need to look at with regard to your suspension?'

'It's a bit more than that, Chief Inspector. I believe I know who it is that has tried to frame me by downloading pornographic images onto my laptop. Do you remember some time back that I had a young computer support civilian by the name of Tim Ridgway working in my department? He was dismissed from the force for accessing PNC without authority. In fact you dealt with his dismissal.'

'I do indeed. What on earth has he got to do with any of this?'

'Well, I believe he took the dismissal very badly and since then he has been planning an act of revenge – and he is the one who hacked into my laptop.'

'But do you have any proof of this?'

'Yes, I certainly do have proof! Here is the image of him accessing my machine,' responded Alan, showing him the captured image.

'Where did you get this? But in any case that doesn't necessarily prove he was the one who downloaded material onto your laptop.'

'No I appreciate that, and it would take too long to explain how I got the image but there is a fair chance he has downloaded material onto the laptop. I realise there has to be more investigative work that needs to be done here but I believe he is the one who set this whole thing up. And, what's more, I believe he is also running a card-skimming scam. I can't go into details on how I know all this – but you must follow it up.'

'Well, sir, you haven't given me much to go on and…'

'Look, these are the contacts and telephone numbers that we found on an ATM skimming device which we believe belongs to him. What more do you want? Do you want me to investigate this for you?' said Alan, angrily cutting him short. 'What is the matter with you people? I'm giving you information here that you can act upon immediately. I bet if this was a murder case you'd soon be following things up.'

'Yes, but fortunately it isn't. Where did you get this card skimming device from?'

Chief Inspector Newton suddenly looked alarmed.

'That's not important at this stage, but rest assured it was obtained from someone who we believe is connected with him.'

'You mention 'we.' Who exactly is the 'we?'

'That's also not important but he is a good friend of mine.'

'This is all very secretive, sir, and you will need to tell us a lot more – and in particular how you came into possession of an ATM skimming device. That in itself is a very serious offence.'

'I can cover all this when you chaps finally get off your arses and start investigating this lead,' replied Alan, whose exasperation with the conversation was clear to see.

At the same time, however, Alan realised that he was on rather dodgy ground here because he still, at this stage, didn't really have the proof that the device had in fact come from Tim Ridgway – and he was now in doubt himself.

'Do you have any further information or evidence or is this it?' asked the Chief Inspector, thinking he'd had a wasted visit.

'No, that's all I have at present but clearly it is worth investigating. Don't you agree?'

'I'll see what I can do, sir, but I'm afraid I can't promise anything,' said the Chief Inspector, getting up to leave.

'I despair at times. Can't you see I'm trying to clear my name here, Chief Inspector, and I'm giving you the information that will lead you to the offender.'

'As I say, sir, leave it with me. I will certainly pass on this information to the team dealing with your case and it will be for them to decide on the next course of action. In the meantime, please do not try and investigate this yourself, sir.'

'Very well, Chief Inspector, thank you for coming. Please see what you can do.'

Alan despondently closed the front door behind him.

**

Tariq Atiq had watched his income go down rapidly over the past few weeks, since Charlie and Tim no longer provided him with card information for cloning. They had found other ways of earning illegal money and they no longer needed him. Tariq now had considerable debts. At the height of his income from illegal card-cloning he had taken out a large personal loan to buy a top-of-the-range sports car. It was his pride and joy but most of his income was taken up now paying for it. He was in arrears and had received demand letters to settle the final balance. He'd ignored these, thinking that his circumstances would change soon. He had even resorted to approaching complete strangers with offers of earning extra cash but most had not even given him the time of day and, in some cases, all he got was abuse. He had never told them about the skimming devices – he kept that back for his chat up line if they showed any remote interest. He'd now decided to start using some of the cloned cards which he had created a while back, even though he didn't know whether they had been blocked or were still valid.

Tariq gathered together about a dozen credit cards and took the train into the city and decided he would draw out a large sum of money to at least start to pay off his debtors. On leaving Piccadilly station he walked down the station approach and entered the first bank he came to, the Swallow National Bank on Portland Street, and decided he would draw out five hundred pounds. He walked up to the cashier in the bank and presented his cloned card. It was still in date and there was no reason to suspect that it was no longer valid.

'I'd like to withdraw five hundred pounds, please,' and he inserted the cloned card into the card reader on the counter.

'Yes, certainly sir. Could you please enter your PIN number,' replied the cashier.

Tariq entered the PIN number which he'd previously written down on the back of his hand.

Unbeknown to Tariq a message had flashed up onto the cashier's screen warning that the card had been stolen and subsequently blocked.

'How would you like the cash?' enquired the cashier, who had pressed a button under the desk and was now stalling for time.

'In fifty pound notes if at all possible,' replied Tariq politely.

'Yes, certainly sir. I just need to get further bank notes from the safe,' replied the cashier, looking into the till. 'I won't be a moment. I'm sorry to keep you waiting.'

Tariq stood waiting nervously for a few minutes and just then he heard the automatic doors behind him close. Before he had even had time to think about what was going on, two managers appeared behind him.

'Could you walk this way sir? We just need to ask you a few questions,' said one of the managers, swiftly removing the credit card from the reader and placing it in his pocket.

Tariq thought about running but there was nowhere to run to. A security officer was already guarding the only exit by standing in front of the locked doors. Tariq was now well and truly trapped. The managers escorted him past the confused queue of customers to an office at the rear of the bank. All he remembered at this point was the door being locked behind him as he sat in isolation for the long wait for the police to arrive.

CHAPTER 34

Alan Jackson was doing his best to keep himself occupied. There was no doubt about it, the spare time he had through his suspension had enabled him to do all sorts of jobs around the house and gardens. On this particular morning he had decided to give his car a full valet on the driveway when his phone rang. He dashed into the kitchen to pick up the phone.

'Good morning. Is that Superintendent Jackson?' said the voice on the other end.

'Yes it is. Who is this calling – and where did you get my number from?'

'I'm Superintendent Hemingway from the National Police Complaints Board. Your phone number is on file, of course. I'm investigating your case and we need you to answer a few questions. Will you be in this afternoon?

'Yes, I'm not going anywhere.'

'Good. Well, shall we say two pm?'

'Yes, that's fine. I'll see you then.'

'I will be accompanied by Inspector Wilbraham who I believe you have already met.'

'I have indeed. I look forward to seeing you later.'

At last we might be getting somewhere, and about time too, he thought as he replaced the receiver and went back outside to finish polishing his car.

***

Tariq Atiq had been sitting waiting in a dimly-lit room at the rear of the bank. He had never been in any trouble with the police before and was wondering how he might concoct some sort of believable story, but, try as he might, he couldn't come up with any form of plausible tale. Just then the door opened and the bank manager arrived, accompanied by two police officers.

'Now then, sir, we understand you have attempted to withdraw funds from a bank account using a credit card that isn't in fact yours. The card in question had been blocked as stolen?' said the first officer.

Tariq just nodded.

'So, firstly, can you provide us with your full name?'

Tariq Atiq thought for a moment. Could he get away with being Dr Giles Stewart? He decided against it.

'Tariq Atiq,' he replied.

'So, you are not Dr. Giles Stewart as it says on this credit card?'

'No.'

'Well, Mr Atiq, I have to tell you that you are now under arrest on suspicion of stealing a credit card and attempting to withdraw funds from someone else's bank account. You do not have to say anything. But it may harm your defence if you do not mention when questioned something which you later rely on in court. Anything you do say may be given in evidence. Do you understand?' said the officer.

'No comment.'

'In that case, sir, we have no option but to take you down to the nearest police station where you will be interviewed further. Do you understand what I'm saying?'

Tariq shrugged his shoulders and refused to co-operate or make any further comment. He was handcuffed by the police officer and taken away, passing a number of shocked bank customers on his way out. He was then bundled into the waiting police car for the short drive to the Midshire Central police station.

***

Alan Jackson waited in patiently for the Superintendent and Inspector to arrive at his home but they were delayed and Alan became more and more frustrated. They eventually arrived at three pm: apparently they had been delayed with traffic on a previous call.

When they did arrive, both officers were in uniform. They parked their unmarked police car in the driveway as Alan, who was now not in the best frame of mind, opened the front door to them.

'I thought you said two pm!' Alan was not going to give them time to make their excuses.

'Yes, sorry about that, Superintendent Jackson. We were delayed at a previous meeting by traffic problems in the city. However, we are here now, so shall we go through?' replied Superintendent Hemingway as he stood on the doorstep.

'Yes, come on in. Please go into the lounge, down the hallway on the left,' responded Alan, trying to lighten up a little.

The two officers went into the lounge and sat in the two armchairs. Alan Jackson decided he would prefer to stand.

'Well, Superintendent, as you know we are investigating your case, and Chief Inspector Newton, we understand, visited you a couple of weeks ago after you had called him and said you had some fresh evidence. He in turn passed this information from his visit onto us and we felt we needed to come over personally to discuss it with you.'

'Yes, that's correct. Good. At long last we might now be getting somewhere. I gave the Chief Inspector the contact details of the people who I believe are involved in setting me up in this dreadful situation. Have you managed to follow any of this up yet?'

'No, not exactly Superintendent – you see we are very concerned that, according to Chief Inspector Newton, you obtained the contact details through a skimming device. Is that correct?'

'Yes, that's correct – but surely how I acquired the details is not important at this stage,' said Alan Jackson, wondering where the conversation was now leading.

'Well, I must inform you, sir, that being in possession of such a device is illegal and you could very well be looking at a lengthy prison sentence if you are found guilty with this in your possession.'

'But that's ridiculous Superintendent. I believe it will lead us to the real culprits of all this.'

'That may well be the case, Superintendent Jackson, but can you tell me who exactly you are referring to as 'we'?'

At this point Alan was very concerned that Midshire Police were not only not treating this new information as he expected but, more seriously, he would have to now give out Jeff's details.

'Look, Superintendent, a good friend of mine helped me investigate this bizarre situation and, to be honest, we have already uncovered far more than you probably have with the progress of your investigation. I am not prepared to tell you his name as it is not relevant.'

'But, Superintendent Jackson, you must realise the situation does not look good for you as it stands. You have money you don't seem to have accounted for which has been transferred into your bank account and you openly admit you have had access to a skimming device. How do we know you are not trying to divert attention to someone else, someone you in fact recommended for dismissal a few months back, i.e Timothy Ridgway?' said Inspector Wilbraham, consulting her notes.

'This is insane! Why on earth would I go to those lengths and risk everything I have worked for? I'm a police superintendent with almost thirty years' service. Why on earth would I risk my entire pension and everything else to get involved in something like illegal ATM skimming and pornographic distribution? Come on, see sense, officer.'

Superintendent Hemingway and Inspector Wilbraham didn't look convinced.

'Now, look, I've had enough of this conversation. If you have no further questions then I'd like you to leave now. I've provided you with all the information on how you can wrap this up quickly and you even have a photograph of the offender.'

'Very well, Superintendent Jackson, we will leave it for now, but rest assured we intend to get to the bottom of all this and we will leave no stone unturned,' replied Superintendent Hemingway as the front door closed behind them.

Alan Jackson waited for them to drive off and he immediately picked up the phone and called Jeff Reynolds.

'Jeff, it's me, Alan. You have to get rid of that skimming device pretty damn quick – as soon as you can. I'll explain why later.'

CHAPTER 35

Tariq Atiq was now sitting in a cell in the Midshire Central Police Station custody suite awaiting further questioning. He had refused to co-operate with the police at the bank and he was now being held for further questioning by detectives. He had been booked into custody and informed of his rights by the custody sergeant and told that he would be formally interviewed later and probably charged with the offence. The police had removed all of his belongings including a dozen cloned credit cards and his mobile phone, which had immediately been passed onto the Hi-Tech crime team for further examination.

After a short while he was eventually escorted towards an adjacent interview room, accompanied by the duty solicitor. There were two police officers there waiting to interview him.

Tariq entered the interview room and sat down and the first police officer switched on the recording device on the desk.

Tariq and the duty solicitor sat at the desk.

'This interview is being tape recorded. I am DS Holdsworth and I am based at Midshire Police. I work for the Card Fraud Investigation team. What is your full name?'

'Tariq Atiq.'

'Ok. Tariq, can you please confirm your date of birth.'

'31st March, 1990.'

'Also present are DC Watkins and Mr Harold Evans-Morris, the duty solicitor. And just to confirm, is it your wish to have the duty solicitor present with you and are you happy for anything to be discussed in front of him?'

'Yes, that's correct,' replied Tariq nervously.

'Ok, Tariq. The date is 13th April 2015 and the time by my watch is 14.45 hours. This interview is being conducted at Midshire Central police station.

'Before you answer I need to formally caution you. You do not have to say anything unless you wish to do so, but what you do say may be given in evidence.'

'No comment.'

'On the morning of the 13th April 2015, between 10.00 and 10.30am, you entered the Swallow National Bank in Portland Street and attempted to withdraw five hundred pounds from the account of Dr Giles Stewart by presenting a credit card of the same name to the cashier.'

'No comment.'

'Can you please tell me where you obtained this particular credit card?'

'No comment.'

'For the purposes of the tape I am now showing Mr Atiq a dozen other credit cards in different names which were found in his possession. Can you explain where you obtained these?'

'No comment.'

DS Holdsworth continued to interview Tariq Atiq who continued to respond with no comment. At the end of the interview he was returned to his cell.

***

Jeff Reynolds was shocked to receive the phone call from Alan Jackson. He couldn't settle after the call, wondering what on earth had happened since Alan had passed the details on to the police.

Alan seemed to be in quite a state when he called and Jeff was concerned by this. Nevertheless, Jeff was determined now to hand back the skimming device as soon as possible. They had got all the information they needed from it and it was now time to get rid of it.

He rang the number he had for Suma but the call directly diverted to his voicemail. Jeff left a message asking him to return the call as soon as possible.

It didn't take long and it must have only been a few minutes later when Jeff's mobile rang.

'Hello, Jeff Reynolds here. Is that you, Suma?'

'Yes, this is Suma. How can I help you?' replied the voice on the other end, clearly going along with the conversation.

'Suma, can we meet up again? I need to give you back the skimming device. We've finished with it and no longer have any further use for it.'

'Ok, no problem. We can meet up. Do you want to suggest a place to hand it back?'

'Well, how about the Jelly Bean café? Shall we say tomorrow evening at 8pm? It should be quiet then,' replied Jeff, thinking it somewhat strange that Suma asked where to meet.

'Yes, that's fine. I'll see you then,' said the voice.

***

DC Hodgson and DC Heath had decided it was about time they followed up the Robinson family and were travelling in Jack Hodgson's car together to Biddulph to interview them.

'I'm really glad you could join us, Clive. It's been a long time since we worked together and, to be honest, it would have been quite a steep learning curve for us taking on the card fraud cases without you,' said DC Hodgson as he drove down the A500 towards Stoke-on-Trent.

'No problem, Jack – it's a pleasure to be working with you and Ted Wilson again. Not sure why you've chosen this route to Biddulph, though! You never did have any sense of direction! You need to leave at this next junction, signposted Tunstall.'

'Don't you start, Clive! I have enough earache from the missus on my sense of direction. It's a good job you're with me. I'm lost around these parts! I just follow the sat-nav these days.'

They continued for several miles past the old disused Chatterley Whitfield Coal Mine and shortly after they took a turning to the right and drove up a steep un-adopted road leading onto a farm track. They soon arrived at a row of cottages which looked as though they had originally belonged to a nearby farm.

'Well, this must be the place. The views are wonderful,' said DC Hodgson. 'I just hope they're in. It's tea time so I guess they should be. I didn't want to alert them that we were coming.'

They parked the car next to a Volvo estate across the lane from the terraced cottages and walked up to number 48. DC Heath rang the doorbell and they could hear quite a bit of movement in the hallway. Eventually a girl aged about nine years came to the door.

'Oh, hello. Is your mother or father in?' asked DC Heath.

'Yes, they are both in. Who shall I say is calling?' said the girl politely.

'We are from Midshire Police,' responded DC Heath.

'Ok, just wait here please. I won't be a moment,' and she went off down the narrow hallway.

It was minutes later when Mrs Robinson arrived at the front door.

'Hello, can I help you?' said Mrs Robinson, looking concerned. 'Is there anything wrong? Lucy said you were police officers.'

'No, nothing to worry about, Mrs Robinson. Can we please come in? We just need to ask you a few questions,' responded DC Hodgson, showing his warrant card.

'Oh – please come in.'

They made their way down the narrow hallway into a larger than expected back room. The room was somewhat sparsely furnished with just a three piece suite, television and coffee table. On the mantelpiece above the open fireplace was a collection of framed photographs. The three children were all sitting quietly watching a children's television programme.

'Children, would you mind going out to play in the garden while I talk to these gentlemen.'

The three children got up from watching the television and without any protest went straight out to play into the back garden. Mrs Robinson switched off the television in the corner.

'Please sit yourselves down, officers, and tell me how I can help you.'

'We are following up some enquiries. I must stress there is nothing to worry about, Mrs Robinson. But first, can you please tell me how long you have lived here?' enquired DC Hodgson.

'We moved here about two months ago.'

'And before that?'

'We were living with my mother in Bolton.'

'I see,' said DC Hodgson. 'And what brings you to the area?'

'Well, it is my husband's job. He works as a lorry driver for one of the large supermarkets and is now based around here.'

'Is your husband at home?'

'Yes, he is but I'm afraid he is sleeping upstairs. He is on permanent nights at present and I don't really want to wake him. He really needs his sleep, as I'm sure you can imagine.'

'Of course, I understand. Tell me, have you lived in Crewe at any time?'

'No, like I said, we lived in Bolton before coming here.'

'What is your husband's full name, Mrs Robinson?'

'It's John Edward Robinson.'

'And his date of birth?'

'27th April, 1970.'

'And your full name and date of birth?'

'June Elisabeth Robinson. 30th August, 1972.'

'Ok. Thank you for the information, Mrs Robinson,' said DC Hodgson, making further notes.

'Can you tell me what all this is about?'

'We are just conducting routine enquiries. There is nothing to worry about, I assure you.'

DC Heath picked up one of the photographs on the mantelpiece and casually asked, 'Is this your family?'

'Yes, these are our three children, Daniel, Emily and Lucy, playing in the garden with their grandma in Bolton.'

'Nice children, Mrs Robinson, and well-behaved. You must be very proud of them. Thank you for all your help. I think that will be all. We are sorry to have troubled you. We'll see ourselves out.'

As DC Hodgson and DC Heath closed the front door behind them and climbed into DC Hodgson's car, they didn't see the curtains move slightly in the upstairs window.

'Well, the family seemed quite kosher, Clive. It looks like we are back at square one,' sighed DC Hodgson as he drove through the Biddulph town centre. 'Although we need to check out if we have anything on either of them. They did seem quite genuine, I thought.'

'Hmm, I'm not so sure, Jack. You know that family photograph that I picked up?'

'Yes.'

'Well, the old lady in it looked familiar to me. Now I wonder where I've seen her before. I just can't seem to place her.'

**

Jeff Reynolds made sure he'd got everything back together again after disassembling the skimming device. He'd carefully parcelled up the device together with the pin pad overlay and then set off to catch the train into the city centre. As it was now pouring with rain he decided to take a cab from Piccadilly station to the Jelly Bean café. It was mid-week and the cafe was quiet, as he'd expected. He looked at his watch. He'd arrived five minutes early and couldn't wait to offload the package back to its owner. He ordered himself a coffee and took a seat by the window to watch out for Suma. He'd only been there for a few minutes when a stranger approached him and took him quite by surprise.

'Are you Jeff Reynolds?' said the stranger.

'Yes, that's right,' responded Jeff, looking somewhat startled.

'Suma sends his apologies – he couldn't make it. I've come to collect the skimming device which I believe you have brought back.'

'Oh, right, yes – it's here,' said Jeff, handing him the package from inside his jacket and feeling somewhat relieved that he could now finally hand it over. 'It's all in here. We have now finished with it.'

The stranger took one look inside the package and signalled to another man whom Jeff hadn't seen waiting in the doorway.

'Ok, Mr Reynolds. My name is DC Watkins. You are now under arrest on suspicion of stealing credit card information and also being in possession of a skimming device. You do not have to say anything. But it may harm your defence if you do not mention when questioned something which you later rely on in court. Anything you do say may be given in evidence. Do you understand?' he said, flashing his warrant card.

Jeff was, for once, stuck for words. His heart was racing. He opened his mouth but nothing came out.

'Finish your coffee, Mr Reynolds – and we would then like you to come down with us to the police station,' said DC Watkins.

CHAPTER 36

The Hi-Tech Crime Unit in Midshire Police was as busy as ever with an increased workload of computers, laptops, cameras and a host of other digital devices to forensically examine. Due to the recent cutbacks in headcount the force still only had three technical support technicians to examine and report on the contents of the various devices that were regularly seized as evidence during investigations.

John Barry was the civilian head of the unit and had just received Tariq Atiq's mobile phone from DS Holdsworth. He had already contacted the force SPOC unit to obtain the call records for that particular number. Obtaining the call records from the service provider had to be approved and signed for by a senior officer and could possibly take some time. He was therefore getting on with the task of examining Tariq's mobile and was in the process of downloading the contacts, call log and any images found on it. To his surprise, there was a limited set of contacts, namely, thunderbird2, thunderbird3, jh and wk.

Two of the contacts had associated images attached so he downloaded these onto his laptop and ran them through the force facial recognition system. They came back with no exact matches so he decided to print them and added them to his interim forensic report. He added the contact phone numbers to the local intelligence system and linked them to Tariq Atiq's intelligence record.

Once the call records came back from the SPOC team these would be passed to the analyst working on DS Holdworth's team. He decided that he had taken this as far as he could at this stage and contacted DS Holdsworth by email, who was quick to respond.

Hi Jim. I've had a quick look at this mobile phone belonging to Tariq Atiq. There isn't much to go on, to be honest and I've requested for the call records to be sent to me which I will forward on, but what I have got is the contacts and a couple of associated facial images. I've printed these off and attached them to the report. I did a quick check on the images but there isn't an exact match from the facial recognition system. It could be the quality of the images as they were of course taken on the mobile phone and it could be down to lighting problems. Anyway, I'm emailing it over to you now. I'll give you a call when I receive the call records.

Regards
John.

Thanks, John. I appreciate your help. You must be very busy. We haven't charged Tariq Atiq yet. We're holding him in custody at present and I suspect he is going to lead us to a number of other arrests. I look forward to reading your interim report. I will also keep you posted on any other developments.

Regards
Jim.

***

Jeff Reynolds was taken by car to Midshire Central police station, with which he was very familiar, as it so happened. It was where he had installed a number of systems when he was a support technician before he retired. He was well-known to a number of the staff who still worked there and they were surprised to see him in the corridor being escorted into one of the interview rooms.

He was shown into the interview room by DS Holdsworth and DC Watkins.

As he entered the room and sat down with the two detectives he was offered a cup of tea which he declined. DS Holdsworth switched on the tape recorder and opened the interview.

'This interview is being tape recorded. I am DS Holdsworth and I am based at Midshire Police. I work for the Card Fraud Investigation team. What is your full name?'

'Jeffrey Eric Reynolds.'

'Can you please confirm your date of birth.'

'30th March, 1958.'

'Also present is DC Watkins. The date is 15th April, 2015 and the time by my watch is 22.45 hours. This interview is being conducted at Midshire Central police station. Before you answer, Mr Reynolds, I need to formally caution you. You do not have to say anything unless you wish to do so, but what you do say may be given in evidence.'

'I understand.'

'On the evening of the 15th April 2015 between 8pm and 9pm you entered the Jelly Bean café off Oxford Road, Manchester and you were in possession of an ATM card skimming device.'

Jeff Reynolds nodded.

'For the purpose of the tape the defendant nodded in agreement. So can you please tell me where you obtained this device?'

'Yes. I was returning it to the person I'd rented it from.'

'How much had you paid to rent the device?'

'Five hundred pounds for six weeks.'

'And what is the name and address of this person who you say rented you this device?'

'All I know is that his name is Suma. I met him in the Jelly Bean Café a few weeks ago. I don't have any details other than his mobile phone number.'

'Do you have an address for this person called Suma?'

'No.'

'Are you seriously telling us that you rented this equipment from someone who you met in the Jelly Bean Café, a complete stranger?'

'Yes, that's correct.'

'Does the name Tariq Atiq mean anything to you?'

'No.'

'Have you installed this device in any ATMs since you received it?'

'No.'

'So why were you returning it? Had you changed your mind about using it?'

'I never had any intention of using it.'

'Come on, Mr Reynolds! Do you really expect us to believe that? Why on earth would you pay to rent such a device and not use it?'

'It was part of an investigation that I was conducting.'

'What sort of investigation was that then? Into what exactly?'

At this point Jeff Reynolds realised he had no option but to divulge everything on how and why he had come into possession of the skimming device – and DS

Holdsworth and DS Watkins were somewhat shocked by his response.

'A good friend of mine, whom you will both know, is a police Superintendent who is currently suspended from Midshire Police. His name is Alan Jackson and we both believe he is being framed for something he most definitely did not do, in that he was allegedly storing and selling online pornographic material. We still believe the person who rented the skimming device would lead us to the person behind all this.'

'You said that the name of the person you rented the device from was Suma?'

'That's correct, but I think the person who owns the device is Tim Ridgway, and he is the one framing Superintendent Alan Jackson.'

'So how exactly would this lead you to this person behind Superintendent Jackson's case?'

'The device includes an embedded SIM card which we have extracted and passed the details on to Midshire Police.'

'When was this?' said DS Holdsworth, looking somewhat surprised.

'Alan Jackson provided these details to Chief Inspector Newton in your Professional Standards Department a couple of weeks ago. I suggest you speak to him. He will verify this.'

DS Holdsworth looked across at DC Watkins, who was shrugging his shoulders on hearing this information.

'We will check out your story, but, as far as we are aware, Chief Inspector Newton has not reported this,' said DS Holdsworth.

'I cannot be held responsible if your departments are not communicating with each other, can I? I mean, how can you ever expect to have joined-up justice systems when you don't even communicate internally?' argued Jeff Reynolds.

'That will be all for now, Mr Reynolds. We will need to speak to you again soon but in the meantime you will be released on bail. You are free to leave and we will be following up on what you have told us with Chief Inspector Newton.'

***

John Barry from the Hi-Tech Crime unit had received the call records from Tariq Atiq's mobile and these had been loaded into the investigation system, together with the SIM data, by Richard Evans, the analyst working on Operation Trident. John's team were now also examining the skimming device that had been taken from Jeff Reynolds at the Jelly Bean café.

They too had discovered the embedded SIM card that Jeff Reynolds and Joe Smithson had found in the skimming device and the contact data from this had also been downloaded into the investigation database. But they had also discovered something else in the device, something that Jeff and Joe had missed. There was a shadow file of pre-encrypted credit card details from when the skimming device had been used before. This was the file of credit card captured transactions which would be encrypted and transmitted to the SIM card contact. John Barry decided to also load this into the investigation database and, rather than wait for the overnight triggering run to take place, he invoked the Midshire Police database comparison which would cross-check all data held in different systems and report when matches were found.

Within minutes the report burst onto John Barry's computer screen and, to his amazement, there were a number of matches found in other systems.

**

DC Hodgson was holding his weekly review with his team.

'We are no nearer locating this Polish family who left the Crewe area. For all we know they could be living back in Warsaw. Yet, I seem to think they are still in the country,' said DC Hodgson, addressing the team.'

'Can I just say something, Jack?' requested DC Heath, who was sitting back with his arms folded.

'I've been racking my brains on that family photograph that we saw at the Robinson's house in Biddulph yesterday. I couldn't think where I had seen that old lady in the photograph before and then it dawned on me. If you recall, the photograph on the mantelpiece was of the three children playing in the garden.'

'Yes, I remember the photograph – but what of it?'

'Well, Mrs Robinson told us that it was of the children playing at their grandma's house in Bolton.'

'And it probably was. Why wouldn't it be?'

'Well, I don't think it was in Bolton – and, if you recall, the old lady was pictured throwing a ball into their garden. It would not have been their grandma on the other side of a neighbour's hedge, would it – unless she'd nipped over the other side? I remembered afterwards where I had seen her before. She was the old lady in Antrobus Street, Crewe, the old lady next door – and, looking at my notes, I think her name is Mrs Morris. The Robinson family have been living in the Kolowskis' house!'

'Absolutely brilliant, Clive! I think we may have found our family!'

CHAPTER 37

PC John Wilson, due to an injury, had been seconded from operational duties to the Incident Monitoring section at force HQ. It was his job to monitor the triggering reports that appeared each morning from the overnight processing run. The Triggering system was the corner stone of the new Midshire crime system, where names, vehicles, phone numbers, addresses, you name it, were automatically checked for multiple occurrences across all the force databases. All too often in the past, officers may not have been aware of records or the presence of individuals who were being investigated in other incidents. The triggering system overcame all that by automatically alerting officers. PC Wilson was reviewing the latest report when he spotted a fixed penalty notice for a vehicle that was also on a stolen vehicle incident. He checked the stolen vehicle record and contacted the last person who had updated the record.

'Hello. DC Hodgson speaking. How can I help you?'

'Ah, good afternoon Jack. It's John Wilson from Incident Monitoring here. Long time no speak.'

'Hi, John – good to hear from you! Yes, it's been a while! So they've moved you into HQ, then, a nice cushy number?'

'Yes, that's right, Jack. It's certainly better than pounding the beat in the middle of a cold night!'

'You can say that again! I don't want to go back to that again.'

DC Hodgson and PC Wilson had worked together as uniformed officers in 'A' division on the same shift and they had gone their separate ways when Jack had been transferred into CID.

'It's really good to hear from you. Don't tell me, John, you are finally retiring and you are inviting me to your leaving do! You know me, I always enjoy a good piss up!'

'I wish. No, nothing like that, Jack. I've still got a few years left in me yet. I'll tell you, the reason for my call is that the triggering system has picked up a vehicle with a fixed penalty notice and alerted us to the fact that it's stolen and being investigated on Operation Carousel. I thought you should know, as you appear to be the record owner on the system.'

'Well, I'm no longer involved in Operation Carousel because the NCA have taken over the investigation, but I'm interested to know which vehicle registration and any associated details?'

'It's a Silver Ford Mondeo saloon, registration JX12YUV. The owner was given a fixed penalty notice for speeding on the M6 last week.'

'Did you say JX12YUV John? Are you sure it wasn't red and not silver?'

'Yes, I'm looking at the camera images. It's most definitely a silver Mondeo saloon, JX12YUV.'

'But I remember that registration – that was one we were investigating, but it was red.'

'Well this one's definitely silver. I haven't checked PNC. I mean, there's only so much time in the day! You know how it is these days.'

Suddenly DC Hodgson thought that surely they wouldn't be stupid enough to use the same vehicle registration for cloning other vehicles, regardless of colour.

'If you check on PNC, John, you will find the colour of that registration is red and it belongs to Northern Computer Services,' said DC Hodgson.

'Well, do you have a name for a contact in the National Crime Agency who is now dealing with this so I can inform them?' asked PC Wilson.

'No, but leave it with me. I'll pass the details on to them. Can you give me the name and address of the driver?'

'Ah, well, therein lies another problem Jack! Yes, we do have a name and address – but we haven't been able to trace the driver. It looks as if he's provided a false name, Francisek Balinski. He gave us an address of 27 Antrobus Street, Crewe and he hasn't yet presented his documents.'

'Did you say 27 Antrobus Street, Crewe?'

'Yes! And that's another thing. The Triggering system also alerted us to the fact that the address has also been previously recorded as part of the Operation Trident investigation. I haven't spoken to those guys yet. I'm not sure how that is even connected.'

'Well, blow me down, surely not!' shouted DC Hodgson.

'Pardon?'

'Oh, nothing, John – just thinking out loud. Leave it with me – and thanks for the information. And, by the way, I'm working on Operation Trident now myself. I'll pass this on to them. In the meantime, can you just record no further action and please refer any updates to me?'

***

Tim Ridgway had not heard from Tariq now for well over two weeks and he thought it strange as, despite the fact their relationship had suffered recently, they were at least still on speaking terms. He called Tariq's mobile which went straight to an answering service. He switched the phone off immediately without leaving a message.

He decided to ring Charlie to see if he had heard anything.

'Hi, Charlie! Have you heard from Tariq recently? He seems to have disappeared off the face of the earth. He doesn't answer his calls and his father doesn't seem to know where he is and he is also concerned for him. He told me he didn't want to alert the police in case they came snooping. I'm getting a bit worried about his safety, Charlie. I just wondered if you've seen him down the Jelly Bean at all lately?'

'I haven't heard anything, Tim, since I saw him a while back in his shop when I took him that skimming device. I tell you this, though, I'm more worried that he has a skimming device of ours. If that gets into the wrong hands we are well and truly sunk,' said Charlie, thinking only of himself.

***

DCs Hodgson, Heath and Bradley were in the office early and were deep in conversation as to the direction of their next lines of enquiry on the phantom card investigation. Jack had updated his team on the telephone call he had received from PC John Wilson and they were intrigued by the new information they had received.

'Pete, can you follow up on the fresh information we have on this fixed penalty notice that John Wilson told us about? We need to know the details, and, in particular, where and when it was issued. It could well lead us to a different location, of course,' said DC Hodgson.

'Will do, Jack. Leave it with me.'

'What I can't understand, Clive, is this. If this is the family who did a runner from Crewe, then they must have rented it from Wojek Kolowski, who took the mortgage out on the property in the first place. They could possibly hold the credit cards in that same name. There is something not right here. Could John Edward Robinson, Wojek Kolowski and this Francisek Balinski bloke who has just emerged on the scene, all be the same person?'

'I've been thinking that myself, Jack. I think it's about time we paid another visit to see the Robinson family.'

'I agree, Clive – and, this time, we need to speak to Mr Robinson himself and get him out of bed if need be.'

DC Hodgson was just closing his briefcase when DS Holdsworth came storming into the office.

'Have you seen this, Jack?' shouted DS Holdsworth excitedly as he waved a report. 'I've just received this from John Barry. We are definitely onto something here, guys. This is the triggering report from the Hi-Tech Crime unit and if you haven't seen it then you'd better brace yourself for some interesting information.'

'Is it about 27 Antrobus Street, Crewe and Francisek Balinski, sarge?' chuckled DC Hodgson.

'Bugger! How on earth did you know that, Hodgson? I've only just received the report this very minute,' said DS Holdsworth.

'It just shows the system's working, sarge! Yes, we are on to it and Clive and I are just off to pay another visit down to Staffordshire. We'll see you later!'

DC Hodgson grinned as he picked up his coat and headed out of the door.

.

CHAPTER 38

Jean Price had decided to create a fresh case workfile on the telephone analysis aspects. She first loaded all the call records from Tariq Atiq's mobile phone into the link analysis database and then loaded in all mobile numbers and associated call data from Operation Carousel. Finally she dealt with the call records and the contact data from the skimming device SIM card. The data importing process was quick and the software had soon calculated and automatically drawn all the connections between the data. Jean converted the link chart and she didn't have to wait long to see an impressive timeline chart showing callers and connections together with the direction and duration of the calls. But there was one set of connections that stood out a mile – there, bang in the middle of the chart, were several calls made between Tariq's mobile and the mobile number that Frank Renwick had dialled to purchase the Ford Mondeo in Dumfries.

***

It was 10.30am and DC Hodgson and DC Heath had now arrived at Westbrook Terrace, Biddulph, to interview the Robinson family. It had been raining heavily in the night and the farm track leading to the row of houses had become somewhat waterlogged. They parked up and tiptoed their way across the muddy lane to number 48.

'Well, if he's on nights and in bed, he hasn't drawn the curtains yet,' murmured DC Heath, looking upwards as he knocked on the front door.

'He could be sleeping in the back room, of course,' observed DC Hodgson.

'Yeah, maybe you're right,' replied DC Heath.

After a few minutes Mrs Robinson came to the door.

'We are sorry to trouble you again, Mrs Robinson, but we need to ask you and your husband a few more questions,' said DC Hodgson, showing his warrant card as a reminder.

'Oh... can't it wait, officer? John is in bed at the moment,' whispered Mrs Robinson. 'I can't disturb him. You see he needs to sleep after he's been on a long night shift.'

'We won't keep him long and we really do need to speak to both of you at the same time,' explained DC Heath.

'Is this really necessary?' replied Mrs Robinson, changing the tone of the conversation.

'I'm afraid so, Mrs Robinson. Please go and tell him,' instructed DC Hodgson, who had now taken a seat in the armchair.

'Very well, but I'm telling you, he won't be happy with this,' responded Mrs Robinson, as she went off up the stairs.

Minutes later – and to their complete surprise – John Robinson appeared. He was a large, six foot three inches, stockily-built man, dressed smartly – and he certainly didn't look as if he had just woken up or, for that matter, been working overnight.

'So, what's all this about then? Hasn't my wife answered enough of your questions?' he complained angrily.

'Sorry to disturb you, Mr Robinson, but we need to ask *you* in particular a few questions this time,' said DC Hodgson. 'Can you please tell us your previous address before you moved here?'

'What is the matter with you lot! My wife has already told you, we were living with my mother in Bolton,' he said sharply.

DC Heath remembered that Mrs Robinson had said it was *her* mother they were living with but decided just to make a mental note of it for the time being.

'And what was that address, sir?'

'Erm, Coleville Street, Bolton, erm… 23,' he replied hesitatingly.

'Do you own or rent this house, sir?' enquired DC Heath, who just then noticed that June Robinson's hand was starting to shake somewhat.

'We rent it. Why, what's wrong with that?' snapped John Robinson. 'Is it against the law?'

'And your landlord's name?'

'Erm, Jones, Michael Jones, I think.'

'Does the name Wojek Kolowski mean anything to you?'

'No, nothing at all. Should it?' shrugged John Robinson, shaking his head.

'Does the name Francisek Balinski mean anything to you, Mr Robinson?'

'No, never heard of him. Who is he?'

'Well, you should have! He is, in fact, the person who has taken out the mortgage on this property. He is, in fact, your landlord.'

It was then that June Robinson broke down in tears.

'You are going to have to tell them, John. We can't keep on doing this; we can't keep living a lie.'

'Be quiet, woman! You don't know what you're talking about. Leave this to me.'

'Keep doing what, exactly?' said DC Hodgson.

'You will have to tell them, John! We can't keep running like this. It's not fair on the children. They are already suffering in school.'

'Be quiet, woman! I told you to leave this to me.'

'Oh for god's sake, John, if you won't tell them then I will,' said June Robinson.

She turned to the two detectives.

'We have been leading double lives, officer. Yes, we did live in Crewe and we do know Wojek. We ran up credit card bills deliberately, then we left there overnight and moved here.'

Immediately John Robinson leapt across the room and grabbed hold of his wife by the arm. 'Oh, you stupid woman! You've done it now! Can't you see? We'll go to prison for this – and then where will the children be?'

'I don't care anymore,' she shouted. 'I just want to put all this behind us. We can't keep doing this! You know very well we were bound to be caught one day – and if it wasn't this, it would have been the cars.'

'What about the cars?' exclaimed DC Hodgson, pricking up his ears.

'We've also been involved in a hire car theft scam, officer,' replied June Robinson, as she wriggled her way free from her husband's grasp. 'It started as a one-off, but it's now got completely out of hand. I didn't want anything to do with it – but they wouldn't listen to me.'

'You stupid, stupid bitch! Now see what you've done.'

John Robinson was now slumped in an armchair.

DC Hodgson couldn't believe what he was hearing. He'd always thought the card enquiry was somehow linked, but here he was, listening to confessions related to both investigations.

'Right, Mr and Mrs Robinson, we have heard enough. We need to take you to the police station for questioning. I have to tell you that you are both now under arrest on suspicion of fraud and theft of motor vehicles. You do not have to say anything. But it may harm your defence if you do not mention when questioned something which you later rely on in court. Anything you do say may be given in evidence.'

'But what about the children? We need to be back for them,' cried June Robinson.

'We need to take you into the nearest police station for further questioning, Mrs Robinson. I'll make sure you are either back in time to collect them from school or at least make arrangements for someone to look after them.'

***

DS Holdsworth and DC Watkins were planning their next move in apprehending the other players involved in the ATM scams.

'We need to wrap this lot up pretty smartish, Clive, before the word gets out that we have Tariq Atiq in custody,' said DS Holdsworth. 'Now we have associated mobile numbers, we have links to the vehicle thefts and we also have a few images – although the facial recognition system doesn't seem to have any possible matches on our database.'

'We also have the likely location where Tariq Atiq spent quite a bit of his time, sarge,' said DC Watkins. 'If my hunch is correct, I think the Jelly Bean café could well be their regular meeting place and is worth another visit, but this time with Tariq's mobile phone, if you get my drift. In fact I suggest we send a text beforehand to the contact numbers we have on the phone – apart from Jeff Reynold's number of course – saying that we need to meet urgently at the Jelly Bean, 8pm prompt. What do you reckon?'

'Great idea. Now, not all of them will respond of course, but I'm sure someone will take the bait. If we could pick up either Thunderbird2 or 3 that would be a great start!' said DS Holdsworth, who had already started preparing to send the text messages from Tariq's mobile.

***

DC Hodgson and DC Heath had booked the only interview room available in Biddulph police station for the initial interview with John and Jean Robinson and they had received back-up support for the interview process.

Jean Robinson was the first to be interviewed and she was keen to tell the officers everything she knew. She was so relieved to pour out every possible detail. She just wanted to see an end to the whole sorry saga. DC Hodgson led the interview and they soon discovered the seemingly endless trail of fraud that the Robinson family had been heavily involved in over the past two years.

'So, Mrs Robinson, are you seriously telling us that this has been going on for some years and no one even noticed that you were moving in and out of properties?' enquired DC Hodgson. 'I can't believe it. I mean, didn't the education system alone alert anyone when you were moving the children from school to school? Is it true that you actually moved properties and locations every few months?'

'That's right, officer. I know it seems crazy, but at first it was so easy. Then it just got out of hand. We could easily hire cars, garage them for a few weeks and resell them on as other registered vehicles. It was only in the last twelve months when John met Wojek in a pub that we hit on the idea of setting up schemes to buy property under false names and then hit the credit cards big time.'

'Well, you certainly did that all right,' piped up DC Heath. 'So, who else is involved in these so-called schemes?'

'Just the four of us; John, Wojek and James.'

'Who is James, do you mean James Smith?'

'No, James Halliday, he's a friend of John's and he does the driving and organises the on-going sales of the vehicles.'

Suddenly DC Hodgson realised that James could be the young man who sold the car to Frank Renwick.

'Would this be James by chance?' he asked, swivelling his laptop round for Mrs Robinson to view the image captured from the CCTV.

'Yes, that's James Halliday all right. There's no mistaking him. I don't know what he's doing involved in all this, his family is loaded. You must have heard of Sir Cuthbert Halliday, he is James's father.'

'It takes all sorts, Mrs Robinson, and your part in this was what, exactly?'

'I hired some of the vehicles and drove them to lockups and garages.'

'So did you also buy duplicate credit cards?'

'No, definitely not – that was James's idea. He came up with that idea as he had a contact in the city. I had nothing whatsoever to do with those.'

'And who exactly is Francisek Balinski, then? Apart from being your current landlord, of course.'

DC Heath was frantically scribbling in his notebook.

'He's Wojek. He uses different Polish names to apply for the mortgages. It so happened he used his own name for the property in Crewe.'

'Did Wojek live with you?'

'Good god, no! Wojek shares a house in Middlewich with his own family. He did all the organising of properties and bank accounts and so on. We moved into each house for a relatively short period.'

'So, there is no Francisek Balinkski then?' asked DC Hodgson.

'Not as far as I am aware. Those were just names that were used with forged paperwork to support them. You'd have to ask John about that.'

'Oh, we will, Mrs Robinson, we will indeed.'

CHAPTER 39

DC Watkins and DS Holdsworth made their way down Oxford Road and arrived at the Jelly Bean Café half an hour before the meeting that had been arranged by text. They ordered themselves coffee, opened up their newspapers and took a seat quietly at the table by the window. Two other officers were sitting in an unmarked car just around the corner.

The café was quiet with just a couple of students on their laptops emailing their friends and family.

Just after 8pm a well-dressed young man, whom they recognised from one of the photographs on Tariq's mobile phone, came in. They waited for their moment. They considered waiting a few more minutes just in case some of the other contacts should arrive but eventually decided they should make a move. Looking at Tariq's phone, DS Holdsworth brought up the image of the young man who had entered the café – identified on the phone as Thunderbird 3. He rang the associated mobile number and the young man who was now sitting across from them picked up the call.

'Hi! Charlie speaking. Is that you, Tariq? Where are you? We've been worried that we haven't heard from you for weeks. Tariq! Are you there, Tariq?'

Within seconds DC Watkins and DS Holdsworth had moved towards Charlie's table and, whilst he was still holding the phone, they moved in. 'Hello Thunderbird 3

– or is it Charlie? My name is DS Holdsworth and you are under arrest on suspicion of being in connection with a series of fraud and identity thefts. You do not have to say anything unless you wish to do so, but what you do say may be given in evidence.'

Charlie was stunned. He knew he couldn't make a run for it as he was well and truly cornered.

'You now need to accompany us to the nearest police station to assist us with our further enquiries.'

The two officers then escorted a shocked Charlie out to the waiting police car but neither officer had noticed Alan, the owner of the Jelly Bean, at the counter sending an urgent text to someone.

***

DC Hodgson and DC Heath had completed their interview with June Robinson, who was still being held in custody. Arrest warrants had been issued to arrest Wojek Kolowski and James Halliday. They were now interviewing June's husband. This was not as easy as the interview with June because John Robinson at first refused to co-operate with the investigation. It was only when he realised that his wife had told them everything that he knew the game was up and realised it was futile not to co-operate. DC Hodgson led the interview with DC Heath taking additional notes.

'So, Mr Robinson, we've told you what your wife has disclosed to us so you may as well come clean. Can you tell us, where exactly did you get the idea that you could hire cars and steal car identities?'

'I overheard a guy in a pub talking about how easy it was to clone a vehicle. I think he had a friend who had just been released from prison and he had been discussing it whilst inside. It sounded easy and we needed the money badly so we decided to give it a go. Sure enough, it was easy. We knew a guy who could knock up the number plates for us so all we needed to do was to find an identical make and model of the car we had stolen.'

'You say 'we' – who exactly do you mean by 'we?' Who else were you working with on this?'

'Well, it was James's idea, he worked with me for a short while and we decided to do it together. It was weeks later that we met with Wojek, who then also worked with us. He was based back at the supermarket warehouse. At first we did the car cloning but Wojek hit on the idea that we could go for the credit card/property scam as well. So we gave it a go and sure enough earned a few bob from it. It got out of hand. It became a way of life.'

'We presume you mean James Halliday?'

'Ah, you know about James, yes James is a bright lad, university degree, private education the lot. What on earth he was doing working with us lot I don't know. He clearly had a lot of potential.'

'So whose idea was it to start using cloned credit cards?'

'That was James. He had a contact, several in fact and for a few quid we had the means to hire cars under false identities.'

'But surely the hire companies needed to see driving licences for those card holders?'

'Yes, but that was easy. Paper or card versions, Wojek could soon get hold of those.'

'Right, that will be all for now, Mr Robinson. We have warrants issued for Wojek and James Halliday. In the meantime we will continue to hold you and your wife here whilst we prepare charges.'

DC Hodgson closed the file in front of him.

'But what about our children? They will be coming home from school any time now.'

'We have advised Social Services and they will be taking care of your children from now on. You should have thought about that before you got in this mess.'

At this point John Robinson broke down in tears.

***

Tim Ridgway was making his way to the Jelly Bean café for his meeting with Tariq. He was never punctual and so, in an attempt to be on time, he decided to take a taxi from his apartment. He couldn't help wondering what Tariq had been up to in the past few weeks. Why hadn't he been in touch before now? Or had he perhaps just headed back to India for a short holiday? Anyway, he clearly wanted to meet urgently. As the taxi headed down Portland Street he received a text from Alan at the Jelly Bean. Tim went into shock.

'Quick, take me back to the apartment as fast as you can!' he shouted to the taxi driver.

'But we are almost there, pal. I can't turn here, the traffic is too busy.'

'Turn around, quick! I've forgotten something. Come on, I'll double your fare.'

The taxi driver, to the annoyance of the drivers behind him, and without any signalling, did a u-turn across the busy evening traffic while the lights were changing and headed straight back to Tim's apartment. About five minutes later they'd arrived back at the apartment block. Tim paid the taxi driver £50 from a wad of notes he had in his bulging wallet and told him he didn't need his services anymore and he could keep the change.

He shot upstairs to his apartment, grabbed his car keys and headed in the lift to the underground car park. He jumped into his car and thirty minutes later was speeding west on the M56 towards North Wales.

***

DS Webster and DC Pete Bradley were parked up in the supermarket distribution warehouse car park waiting for the return of a particular truck. They didn't have to wait long before the truck in question arrived. They watched the driver park up and lock the vehicle and step out of his cab at the end of his shift. He started making his way across to the office to return his paperwork and keys. The two officers got out of their vehicle and approached him.

'Wojek Kolowski?'

'Yes, it might be, who are you?'

'My name is DS Webster. Wojek Kolowski, you are now under arrest on suspicion of fraud, vehicle and identity theft. You do not have to say anything. But, it may harm your defence if you do not mention when questioned something which you later rely on in court. Anything you do say may be given in evidence. Do you understand?'

Wojek Kolowski was silent and before he could think of anything to say he felt the handcuffs from DC Bradley and was bundled swiftly into the back of the waiting police car.

***

DC Hodgson and DC Heath were now driving down the leafy lanes of Cheshire.

'It must be round here somewhere,' said DC Heath, who was driving the unmarked police car past the large gated private houses.

'It's ironic, Clive, do you know that we were driving down these lanes just a few months ago when we first started investigating Operation Carousel, how crazy is that,' replied DC Hodgson, 'hang on, this must be the place here, on the right.'

They pulled into a tree lined driveway and DC Heath pressed the intercom. After a few minutes a lady's voice answered, 'Not today thank you, we are not expecting anyone.'

'Hello madam, this is Midshire Police, is this James Halliday's address?'

'It is indeed, this is Lady Halliday speaking, but if it's a speeding fine can I suggest you put it in the post and we will deal with it accordingly,' replied the posh voice on the intercom.

'It's not quite as simple as that I'm afraid, we have an arrest warrant on him, can you please open the gate?'

'What, don't be silly, you must have the wrong James Halliday.'

'I don't think so, madam, now can you please let us in?'

To their surprise, with no further conversation the gates swung open and DC Heath drove the car down the curved gravel driveway, passing manicured lawns to the front of the impressive Tudor mansion. Parked outside were a number of luxury vehicles including a Rolls Royce and a brand new silver Range Rover. The two officers were just stepping out of the car when, to their surprise, a young man dashed out in front of them attempting to make his escape across the lawn.

But DC Hodgson was quick to respond and, with adrenalin rushing and before the youth could scale the fence on the edge of the lawn, he was rugby tackled and pinned to the ground.

Now short of breath, he just managed to gasp 'James Halliday, you are under arrest on suspicion of vehicle and identity theft. You do not have to say anything. But, it may harm your defence if you do not mention when questioned something which you later rely on in court. Anything you do say may be given in evidence. Do you understand?'

'Ok, Ok let go of me, the game's up,' shouted James Halliday. 'I knew it was just a matter of time, let go of my arm, you're hurting me.'

'Are you alright, Jack?' asked DC Heath, who had just arrived at the scene.

'Yes, I'll be fine Clive, you never lose it, I just need a few minutes to get my breath back.'

James Halliday made no further attempt to escape and he was quickly bundled into the police car and driven off before his mother had time to get hold of him.

***

A 25 year old man was today charged with using a cloned credit card at a bank in Portland Street, Manchester.

According to Midshire Police, Tariq Atiq was arrested and charged with two counts of card fraud and identity theft.

During a search of Atiq's flat in the city centre, police officers found in excess of a hundred cloned credit cards, a skimming device, card copying machine and printouts detailing a number of bank cards.

Police also seized computer equipment and mobile phones.

***

The UK's Cyber Crime Agency, as part of Operation Omega, has arrested six suspected hackers as part of a focused week against cybercrime. Those arrested are suspected of being involved in a number of cyber-related crimes including card theft, identity theft, fraud and virus, Trojan/Ransomware creation.

The operation was co-ordinated across England, Scotland and Wales by the UK agency in conjunction with specialist officers from Midshire Police.

***

Tim Ridgway had decided that something was definitely not right. In fact something was wrong, badly wrong, but he didn't know what exactly. Since receiving the text from Alan at the Jelly Bean café he hadn't heard a thing from Charlie or Tariq. All the text had said was 'Get out quick.' So he'd decided to do exactly that. He was now well and truly on the run but from what exactly? He had tried ringing Charlie but there was no answer. He was now holed up in a bed and breakfast hotel close to the sea front in Llandudno. He'd not had time to pack and had checked in with no bags whatsoever. His laptops had been left behind, still switched on. All he had was his mobile phone, which he decided to leave switched on just in case Tariq or Charlie tried to contact him.

***

Meanwhile, back at Midshire Police HQ, DS Holdsworth and DC Watkins were now following up on the information that Jeff Reynolds had provided them with earlier. They were also checking the potential links with the Professional Standards Unit and were in discussion with Chief Inspector Newton in his office.

'So, just let me get this straight, sir – you actually have an address for Tim Ridgway which was given to you by Alan Jackson a few weeks ago?'

'Yes, that's right, it's here from my notes with Alan,' replied the Chief Inspector, handing over a two-page document. 'But whether he is still living there I've no idea, to be honest. It was something Alan Jackson told me which I passed onto the investigation team looking into his case. I have to say I thought it wouldn't lead us anywhere. Alan Jackson never got on with Tim Ridgway and I presumed it might be a diversion. In hindsight we should have done more in investigating it, of course. We didn't take him seriously with this.'

'Hindsight is a wonderful thing, sir, but it has been most useful and we'll certainly follow it up. As you say, he may well have left that address. That's all we need for now. Thank you for your time, Chief Inspector. We must leave as, I'm sure you understand, time is now of the essence.'

DS Holdsworth and DC Watkins hurriedly left the PSD office and headed straight over to the address given to them. The city centre was as busy as ever and they resorted to switching on the blues and twos in the unmarked car as they weaved their way through the dense traffic. DS Holdsworth had previously radioed the Hi-Tech Crime Unit to meet them at the executive apartment block. On arrival, with the assistance of the receptionist, they took the lift to the penthouse floor. She unlocked the door and they entered Ridgway's apartment. The police officers and the Hi-Tech Crime unit began to search each room – and, to their surprise, in one of the bedrooms found a bank of four laptops still powered up and connected to the internet.

The Hi-Tech crime unit officers had no difficulty in keeping the devices switched on. They had anticipated that the laptops would be locked down and encrypted, but to their complete surprise even the screensavers were switched off and there were no passwords to overcome. They reset the passwords just in case and removed the laptops for detailed examination at Police HQ.

***

Tim Ridgway had tried again to contact Tariq and Charlie but both mobile numbers went direct to voicemail. He had managed to buy a few toiletries from the corner shop and had now been holed up in his room in the guest house at Llandudno for three days and desperately needed to get out. He had taken all his meals in the hotel and was in fear of even walking round the town but he decided to take a short walk up to the Great Orme. At least he could get some fresh air and work out his next move. He walked down the promenade past the Punch and Judy man who was entertaining quite a large crowd of children and pensioners. He passed the entrance to the pier and soon he was walking through the Happy Valley, a delightfully sheltered hollow on the eastern side of the Great Orme. He thought back to the wonderful times he had had here as a young boy when coming on holiday with his parents. The sun was beating down and there wasn't a cloud in the sky so he decided to rest for a while and enjoy the far-reaching views out to sea. He was so tired he decided to lie down on the grass. He hadn't had much sleep over the past three days and very soon he was sound asleep. He didn't know how long he had been lying there when suddenly he sensed people around him as he gradually awoke.

'Tim Ridgway?' said the voice in an authoritative manner.

'Yes,' said Tim, still half asleep.

'I'm DS Holdsworth and this is DC Watkins. You are under arrest on suspicion of fraud and identity theft. You do not have to say anything. But, it may harm your defence if you do not mention when questioned something which you later rely on in court. Anything you do say may be given in evidence. Do you understand?'

Tim thought about trying to run for it but he was exhausted and realised the game was finally up.

'How did you find me?'

'Oh, that was easy,' replied DC Watkins, as he handcuffed him. 'A combination of mobile phone cell site analysis, a number of possible sightings and good old-fashioned policing. You kindly left your mobile phone on for us. Isn't technology wonderful. We have a car waiting for you down at the promenade.'

CHAPTER 40

The Midshire Police and the UK's Cyber Crime Agency carried out a series of arrests this week of hackers who are suspected to be behind stealing the credit card details of over two hundred people.

The arrests took place in the early hours of Saturday morning and the priority was to ensure that any computers and laptops were seized before they could be shut down.

Cyber teams arrived at an exclusive penthouse apartment in the centre of Manchester armed with the necessary equipment for data capture and discovered a number of laptops, miniature cameras and servers which had been left online. These were eventually removed for digital forensic examination by the Midshire Police hi-tech department.

***

A Manchester man was arrested on June 11th in connection with a number of identities stolen across the North West.

According to Midshire Police, twenty-four year old Charles Ellis was arrested and charged with four counts of identity theft.

During a search of Ellis's apartment in the city centre, police investigators found a number of card skimming devices, pin pads and printouts detailing a number of bank cards.

Police also seized computer equipment and mobile phones.

***

Three men and a woman, charged with conspiring to handle vehicles that had been stolen from across the North West of England, have today been found guilty at Knutsford Crown Court.

Over an eighteen month period, fifteen hire cars were reported as stolen in the Midshire area.

John Robinson, forty-five years old, and his wife June, forty-three years-old, both of Biddulph in Staffordshire, Wojek Kolowski, twenty-eight years old and James Halliday, twenty-five years old, were all charged with conspiracy to handle stolen vehicles after having been linked to the Operation Carousel investigation by Midshire Police. The four also pleaded guilty to fraud and identity theft.

After a lengthy trial at Knutsford Crown Court the Judge, Albert Evans, said it was inevitable that the four would face a lengthy term of imprisonment.

EPILOGUE

Superintendent Alan Jackson was back where he wanted to be, behind his desk in police HQ. After eight months his suspension had been finally lifted and he had his old job back – although the force was still investigating whether he had been in possession of a skimming device. They had discussed long and hard about lifting his suspension whilst investigations continued but Chief Inspector Newton supported Alan Jackson and they allowed him to return to his post. He was now familiarising himself with the various IT projects which the force was implementing when he received an internal phone call.

'Hello sir, DS Holdsworth here. We have someone in the Custody Suite who has asked to see you.'

'Really, I can't think who or why someone would be wishing to see me from custody,' said Superintendent Jackson.

'Well, they do, sir. It's someone you know, apparently. His name is Tim Ridgway. He is in custody and has asked to see you. He wants to apologise to you for putting you through hell for the past eight months.'

'I'll be down there in about ten minutes,' said Alan as he replaced the receiver.

'Samantha, I'm just visiting the Custody Suite. I shouldn't be long. You can reach me on the mobile if you need me urgently,' said Alan as he put on his jacket and headed down to the Central Police Station.

The Midshire Custody Suite was a relatively new purpose-built building which was adjacent to the central police station and was designed to accommodate all arrests in the city area. Alan Jackson decided to get a breath of fresh air and walk down to the station rather than take the short drive. Ten minutes later he entered the secure Custody suite.

'I understand you have a Tim Ridgway here who has asked to see me,' he said to the custody sergeant.

'Ah, yes, Superintendent – we do indeed! I'll bring him through into the interview room. If you would like to wait in there sir. He's a bit distressed, I'm afraid.'

Alan Jackson thought, he'll be more than distressed when I bloody finish with him. He went into the interview room and waited. A few minutes later a slightly dishevelled and unshaven Tim Ridgway was escorted in by a police officer.

'Hello Superintendent, thank you for coming to see me.'

'Hello Tim,' Alan Jackson replied, somewhat frostily. He still couldn't believe what Tim had done, putting him through hell over the past months.

'Can I please apologise for what I have done?' said Tim, his voice faltering. 'I bitterly regret the worry and the pain that I must have put you through. I had no right to do what I did to you.'

'Thank you, Tim. At least you have the decency to apologise. But tell me, why did you do it? What on earth made you go to those lengths? I didn't think we had that bad a relationship before you were dismissed. And the one thing that really does bother me is why were you accessing PNC in the first place?'

'Well, I'm not sure you know about my past, but my parents were killed in a car crash when I was young and ever since that day I have been determined to find the driver who ran into them. It was a hit and run.'

Tim Ridgway was now breaking down in tears. 'He left them dying in the car crash, dying at the side of the road. Can you believe that? The police eventually traced him – and all he got was a two year prison sentence and a three year driving ban. He was released after only twelve months and, although it was years later, I was determined to find him – so I resorted to searching PNC. I never did find him of course. Apparently he'd emigrated. But then I was dismissed from the police. That was the final straw. I felt the whole world was against me. I had no money, no prospects and felt extremely bitter to have lost my job. I could see ways of making easy money and at the same time seeking revenge. I bitterly regret it now and hope you can find it in your heart to please forgive me for what I have done to you. I am so, so sorry.'

Alan Jackson paused while Tim Ridgway, head in his hands, sobbed uncontrollably.

'Well, if it helps Tim, I do forgive you for what you have done. Now I suggest you use the time you are likely to spend in prison to try and think how you can rebuild your life and start again. You have a talent and a skill in computing, so use it wisely. I'll be off now and hopefully our paths won't ever cross again.'

Alan left the room.

Six Months Later

A twenty-five year old Manchester man with no previous convictions has been handed a ten year prison sentence for using stolen bank cards to make fraudulent transactions totalling over £62,000.

Timothy John Ridgway, from Oxford Road, admitted receiving the stolen bank card details as well as a charge of fraud by false representation.

During a search of Ridgway's penthouse apartment in an exclusive part of Oxford Road, Midshire Police found a large number of cloned credit cards and listings of credit card details. Investigators also seized computer equipment, mobile phones and skimming devices.

Judge Kenneth Smythe, QC, told Ridgway that he will spend half the sentence in prison, with the remaining time spent on supervised licence when he is eventually released from custody.

Knutsford Crown Court heard that, following the theft of the bank card details, they were used in excess of forty-one times to make a series of fraudulent transactions amounting to over £62,235.

Crown prosecutor Albert Thomas said there were several victims in the case, all of whom had been fully reimbursed for their losses.

Ridgway is still awaiting trial for hacking into a senior police officer's computer and planting pornographic material.

***

A fifty-five year old former police superintendent and a fifty-seven year old computer technician were given a conditional discharge yesterday at Knutsford Magistrates Court. Alan Jackson, a retired police superintendent with Midshire Police, and Jeffrey Alan Reynolds, pleaded guilty to being in possession of an ATM skimming device. Both defendants were ordered to pay seventy-five pounds costs.